About the author

Janice James used to be the Features Editor of *Woman's Own* and is now its Fiction Editor. Before joining the staff, she was a regular contributor to the magazine. Miss James is the author of the bestselling *The Brothers, Volume 1*

Also by Janice James and available from Sphere Books

THE BROTHERS Volume 1

The Brothers

Volume 2

JANICE JAMES

SPHERE BOOKS LIMITED
30/32 Gray's Inn Road, London WC1X 8JL

First published in Great Britain by Sphere Books Ltd 1974

TRADE
MARK

Set in Intertype Plantin

Printed in Great Britain by
Hazell Watson & Viney Ltd,
Aylesbury, Bucks

ISBN 0 7221 4975 1

CHAPTER ONE

Really, thought Mary Hammond as she looked around the lingerie department, the shopping here is better than in London. Less tiring, too, to have the shops so close together rather than trailing from Regent Street to Knightsbridge then back again to Bond Street in case one had missed anything. She examined some lacy nightdresses with great attention to the hand-finished hems. Swiss. Quite exquisite and relatively reasonable. Just the sort of present for Ann. She made up her mind and summoned the assistant.

Now, she decided as she came out of the store into the diffused pink light of the late afternoon, a cup of tea. She smiled as she crossed the road. Four months and the sight of the policeman on traffic duty in his helmet and Bermuda shorts still amused her. Like the men at cocktail parties in dinner jackets and shorts with knee-length socks. The invitations to meet the Governor's wife when one stood around talking about the latest West End shows, and the laziness of servants. The way the Union Jack was run up outside the Government House each morning. It was all so terribly British. Quite unlike Britain.

The hotel was like a giant, opalescent wedding-cake dropped down by a shimmering blue ocean. She had grown very fond of it during her stay. As she walked towards it, she indulged in the sort of decision with which she passed her time so often lately – should she take tea in her room, in the lounge or by the pool. Did all elderly ladies living alone do this kind of thing? Pretend it was important whether they had tea or coffee, walked along the main road or took a back street? Take hours choosing a book or magazine which they had no intention of reading but needed as proof that they had something to do when they sat by themselves in a bar or restaurant? Perhaps we all do that, she decided. We get to the point when our families are grown up and gone and then we have to pass the time of our lives somehow.

She decided on the pool-side, choosing a seat which caught the westering sun, well away from the blue-rinsed American widow who had plagued her so often with her suggestions that they eat together or take trips to St. George's, the old capital of the island. Mary had taken the occasional drink with her. Anna Louise Abercrombie who had buried three husbands to Mary's one. Who had borne one son to Mary's three. Who now spent her life travelling, trying to find some new interest or experience. But who always went back to Miami where she was with her own kind. Or came here where the tourists were predominantly American.

Mary had felt sorry for her but a little of her company went a long way and her doctor's advice forbade her to indulge in the marathon martini drinking which appeared to take up so much of Anna Louise's time. She was always either dressing for drinks, knocking them back or recovering from them. Mary would sit and sip her sherry, making it spin out as long as decently possible while Anna Louise would become more and more flushed. One night she had berated the son whose praises she had previously sung so loudly to Mary, proclaiming him to be a no-good ingrate who never had time to visit his mother. Then she had started to cross-examine Mary about her family, asked her what she was doing here alone. Shatteringly, Mary had realised that Anna Louise felt sorry for her. Saw her in the same loveless situation as herself. Mary had explained coldly that she was here on doctor's orders for a long rest and that her sons were all devoted to her.

"Madam?" Mary looked up surprised. She was almost dozing off in the heat. The waiter stood by her chair. "You wanted some tea, Mrs. Hammond?" Mary looked at him.

"You know," she said. "I think I'll have a Planter's Punch. Is it too early?"

"It's never too early, madam." He smiled and moved away. Mary smiled after him. He was her favourite waiter and had taken particular care of her, moving her seat, adjusting the parasol. Now why on earth had she ordered a punch? Because, she informed herself sternly, you are not a dying old lady. You feel much better after your rest and you are enjoying yourself.

Her waiter brought the tall, cool glass and she sipped it slowly, savouring the fruity richness. The waiter was now leaning over a young woman opposite, taking her order, smiling and laughing with her. She had noticed the young woman's arrival last week only because she looked so much like Ann, her daughter-in-law. Tall, beautiful, self-possessed. She seemed not to care that she was alone. Perhaps she was waiting for her husband or her lover to join her – the knowledge that she was lovely and desirable lending her superb confidence. Or maybe it was a question of age. Perhaps women in future would be able to travel alone, eat alone, drink alone, without being social lepers. This women's liberation thing probably made them all feel they could do whatever they wanted to do by themselves without the company of a man or a child or a dog to justify their existence.

Ann would behave just like that young woman. Look how she'd scooped up her children and walked out on Brian leaving him to cope by himself. It was he who had been completely disorientated at first. He had almost gone to pieces. She knew he had drunk too much. But whenever she had seen Ann, Ann was bright, lively, apparently happy. Of course, Mary reflected, it was Ann's decision to leave Brian. Nowadays it was the women who left their husbands. Who could afford to leave them.

I wonder whether I would have left Robert if I had known twenty years ago that he was having an affair with Jennifer Kingsley, she asked herself for the thousandth time since her husband's death. And if I had known and threatened to leave him, would he have made the decision to stop the affair. For the sake of the children if not herself? But she hadn't known and the affair had gone on and on and a child had been born. Barbara. Mary would have liked a daughter. She sometimes felt they must be more comforting than sons, becoming friends eventually. She had been disappointed in Brian's choice of a wife. She could never imagine Ann's being close friends ever with another woman, least of all her mother-in-law.

Barbara was a nice girl. The sort of girl she would like as a daughter. Warm, frank, outgoing. Not unlike Robert from what little she had seen of her although frank was perhaps an odd way to describe a man who had not acknowledged the birth of an illegitimate daughter until he had made provision for her in his will. One thousand pounds when she was eighteen and half the estate on the death of Mary. She would wait a long time for that money, Mary had vowed to herself grimly on that terrible day of the funeral. Still, she would inherit her thousand pounds soon and take herself off to art school. Mary was pleased about that. When she was living away from home, she would get to know her better. She must write to Cassell, the family solicitor, and find out when exactly Barbara's birthday fell.

"Mary, I didn't see you. Why didn't you come over?" Anna Louise flopped in the chaise longue next to hers. She was wearing Bermuda shorts and Mary thought again how unbecoming they were to all but the tall and slender.

"I didn't see you," Mary lied.

"You're drinking!" Anna Louise accused her. "And the sun isn't even over the yardarm yet. What a lousy limey trick when I've been drinking tea and pretending to be British. Waiter!" She yelled to the waiter's back. "Same again for Mrs. Hammond and a large scotch on the rocks for me."

Mary burst out laughing. "My dear Mrs. Abercrombie . . ."

"Mrs. Abercrombie! Mary, when are you going to stop that?"

"I'm sorry. Anna Louise. I just suddenly felt like a drink. Anyway I can hardly believe these punches are alcoholic."

"Yes, I know – more like fruit salad gone wrong. But you do know where the expression 'pack a punch' comes from, don't you? And I don't mean boxing." Anna Louise leaned back hardly able to restrain herself from grabbing the glass from the waiter. Mary indicated that he should take away her half-full glass before embarking on her second.

"Any news from home?"

"Maybe by the afternoon post. I've been out all afternoon," said Mary. "Shopping."

"What did you buy?"

"A nightie for Ann. My daughter-in-law. Some of that spicy cologne for my sons. I think David will like it although I doubt whether Edward will. Sherry peppers for myself. I'll make some Bermuda dishes when I get home."

"I had a letter this morning from Wendell." Wendell was Anna Louise's son.

"He's coming out to see me next week."

"But that's wonderful for you." Mary was genuinely pleased.

"Yes. He's bringing his wife and my grandson. You'll be able to meet them, won't you?"

"Oh yes. I have another month before I go back."

"You're looking very well."

"I feel it. And the doctor in Hamilton says I'm doing very nicely."

"Say, tell you what. With your feeling so good and me having my son coming, why don't we go out and celebrate tonight?"

"I really don't know, I'm sure . . ." Mary hesitated. Maybe it was the sun or the rum, she didn't know but she was feeling quite kindly disposed to Anna Louise.

"Come on. We'll go to The Harbourfront and have a great big steak and a few drinks. What do you say?"

"Yes." Mary decided. "But if I'm to drink tonight, I can't finish that, I'm afraid. And I must do something about my hair."

"I'll pick you up in your room about eight?" Anna Louise suggested.

Mary nodded, signed her bill and collected her parcels. Anna Louise signalled to the waiter to bring her another drink.

Mary walked to the desk, and asked for the key to her room.

"Certainly Mrs. Hammond. And you have a lot of mail today." The young man behind the desk smiled at her and handed her a card and three letters.

"Thank you." She smiled at him and went to the lift.

Once in her room, she felt a slight regret that she had accepted Anna Louise's invitation. She would have liked to savour her letters, made them the highlight of her day. Letters from home, drinks at tea-time and dinner was all too much. She looked at them. Which first? The card, of course, was from David. Six lines saying he was well, hoping that she was and promising to write soon "at length". She had had ten such cards since she had come to Bermuda. It was ironic, she felt, that her youngest son, the baby who had arrived when Robert had made his money, established his business, David who had had the best education of her three boys, should be the one who hardly wrote to her. Not from lack of desire but because he could hardly string three sentences together on paper. Whereas Edward, her eldest son, Edward who had left school at fourteen and joined his father in the firm when it was a one-van, one-man business, not the thriving road haulage company it was now, took the trouble to sit down and write pages about the business and what was happening. Dear

Edward. It was his way of showing that he loved her, was sorry he had hurt her.

There had been a few references to Jennifer Kingsley in his letters but nothing to worry about. When he wrote to her about the Hammond Transport Company, he couldn't help but mention the woman. After all, she, too, had done well from the late Robert Hammond's will. A director of the company along with Mary's three sons on a completely equal basis. Robert must have been mad. She could understand his wanting Brian and David in the firm. But why Jennifer Kingsley? And how Miss Kingsley could dare to throw herself at Edward's head the way she had. Well, Edward knew now. There would be no question of any goings-on there while she, Mary, was alive.

There was a letter from Edward. She looked at the strong, slanting handwriting then put it to one side. Edward's letters were the best. She would save it till the last. She opened the letter from Alice Birkett. Alice and John Birkett and she and Robert had been the best of friends since they were newly-married. Tom Birkett had given Robert one of his first big jobs.

Alice wrote about the Townswomen's Guild and her bridge and asked about Bermuda. Would she and Tom enjoy a holiday there? It was a pleasant, chatty letter, somewhat contrived. It was odd how a death changed even one's oldest relationships. John and Alice had been more than kind, plying her with invitations but she felt the strain on Alice's side. What was it? Did she see herself like Mary in a few years' time? A widow who no longer entertained for her husband's business friends, who had to find charities and good works to fill her daytime hours? And she didn't like what she saw? Mary sighed and put it down.

The other letter was from her doctor. He had had a favourable report from her physician here. He was glad she was doing so nicely and advised her to continue taking it easily. What would he say if he knew she had just drunk two Planter's Punches? She grinned and picked up Edward's letter.

It was strange. As she read the letter, she sensed the same tension she had in Alice Birkett's letter. Edward wrote about the business, about the offer Hammonds had made for the adjoining plot of land on which to build a new warehouse, reassured her that Mrs. Wheeler was making sure the house ran smoothly and that he was well fed. Everything was going on oiled wheels, it seemed. And then she came to it. One brief sentence thrown away in a middle of a page as though he hoped she might miss it.

Her hands were shaking when she put it down. So, that was what was going on? And Edward. Poor, dear, honest Edward felt he had to mention it but in such a way that she would not think it important. Well it was important. The most important thing in her life. She reached for the telephone.

"Hello, would you put me through to the bookings clerks please." Her mind was racing as she waited for the connection to be made.

"Oh, hello. This is Mrs. Mary Hammond. Would you make me a reservation on a flight to London. . . . Yes, that's right. I want to arrive about noon on Monday. . . . You'll call me back? Thank you. . . . Yes, I know, it's short notice but something has cropped up unexpectedly. It's essential I be in England on Monday."

CHAPTER TWO

At noon on Sunday, Brian Hammond was still in dressing-gown and slippers, reading the newspapers and drinking his fourth or fifth cup of coffee. Sunday, he had decided, was the loneliest day of the week and not Saturday night despite that song Sinatra used to sing when Brian was a young, single man, obliged to dance occasionally in order to meet girls.

Work filled the week efficiently, very often spilling over into the evening when there was always the chance that this too would be prolonged by David's invitation to join him for a drink. He and his younger brother had become very close since they had been brought into the family business. There was, Brian admitted to himself, a little of the alliance of smaller powers against the bigger, incarnated by Edward, in it. But then, it was right that Edward should be aggrieved by the terms of their father's will. Equal shares for all the brothers and Jennifer Kingsley had been a difficult blow for him to take.

Still, even Edward had mellowed these days. And he and Jennifer would probably be married by now if it weren't for mother. Poor Mother. She had taken a severe blow too. Though she sounded cheerful enough in her letters. He decided to write to her that very day.

He stubbed out his cigarette, stopped and looked at the table in disgust. What a mess. Coffee-cups. Papers. Overflowing ashtray. He pushed the papers into a pile. He hadn't read the financial pages. Normally he read them first but he couldn't face them just yet. There were a lot of troubles at Hammond Transport right now. When he had worked on his own papers, there would be time enough for the business news. He began to plan his day.

First he would wash up. Although he ate out most of the time or ate out of tins if he were home, the house seemed to be full of dirty glasses, cups and ashtrays. The charwoman had made a few remarks lately indicating she felt sorry for him which was annoying, at the same time somehow implying that no-one could expect a woman as beautiful as Mrs. Hammond to put up for ever with a dull stick like himself, which was even more annoying.

What did they do on Sundays – he and Ann? It was difficult to recall – memories were quickly blurred by time and bitterness. There had been the children, of course, and the ritual Sunday lunch; maybe a drive if it were fine or a bit of gardening. Then tea. And it was his day to put the children to bed before he and Ann had a light supper on a tray in front of the television set.

In fact, it had been a pretty dull day even then but the mere presence of other people, the fact that you did nothing in company, proved something either to the world or yourself, he wasn't sure which. It showed that you must be attractive and/or interesting. You passed your life away with other people. No wonder Ann had got up and walked away from it. Maybe she was right to feel afraid of the passing of the days. Not to feel afraid of being alone but to take a chance on something better. Whatever that might be.

Enough of this. Today had still to be planned. He glanced at his watch. Nearly one o'clock and he hadn't bathed or dressed yet. On his way upstairs, he stopped. He had realised something. That was the first time since Ann had left that he had looked at his watch and not automatically thought to himself "Christmas present from Ann last year". Maybe he was making progress if you call the assassination of memories progress. Nevertheless, he was whistling by the time he came downstairs again.

He dialled David's number. It would be pleasant to drive over to Chelsea, have a few drinks in his brother's local, maybe some late lunch in one of those trendy restaurants that mushroomed in the area. The phone rang and rang. Nobody there. He put down the receiver unwillingly. There were no friends of his or Ann's he wished to see. Nor would they want to see him at this time on Sunday. All married, they would be presiding over a joint, doling out pudding, wiping sticky fingers and issuing strict orders to eat up everything on the plate, not to talk with full mouths, not to fidget, to children who would resist but would grow up in their turn to issue the same instructions.

Edward? No. Brian was never totally relaxed with his elder brother. Nor, today of all days, did he want to talk to him.

Their conversation was usually shop and Brian did not wish to talk shop since the part of the shop he was responsible for was finance. Now the expansion plans of Hammonds had got under way, more land was needed. At this very moment, they were negotiating for the land next to theirs and it was Brian's job to raise the money for the purchase. No he wouldn't ring Edward. He had no desire to find out what it was like to be interviewed by the Spanish Inquisition. No Sunday could be *that* boring. He would wait to see Edward at the board meeting the next day.

He dialled David's number again, knowing there would be no answer but giving himself time to think. By the fourth ring, he had decided: a few drinks at the local and a sandwich. Back for a sleep and then he'd try David's number again. As he wasn't at home now, chances were he'd gone out for the day and would be free tonight or he was still in bed with some girl in her flat and would be back tired and hungry and ready for some male company later.

David really pulled the girls. Brian felt embarrassed even thinking in phrases like that. Funny really, how different they all were. As far as he knew, Edward had never had a regular girlfriend. He liked women but it had just been work, work, work since he had left school at fourteen. And now he was besotted by Jennifer Kingsley. Jennifer, the old man's mistress. Not that it was easy to think of her in those terms. She was such a thoroughly nice woman. Quiet, attractive, intelligent, dependable. She must have really loved the old man. She wasn't the sort to have affairs. Not like. . . .

Brian stopped himself. He was about to think. . . . not like Ann and he felt immediately disloyal. Ann wasn't the sort to have affairs either. It was just that she was beautiful, impulsive and headstrong and she liked to enjoy life. That didn't mean she was the sort to have affairs. It was usually the quiet, mousy women who did anyway. No, Ann just liked to be admired and complimented. And he had probably failed her there. He hadn't been able to give her the things she wanted. The new house. She had hated this house. This house that seemed so big to him here alone had been a prison for her. She had not worked since they were married. How could she with Nigel's arriving nine months after the wedding and Carol two years later? So all she had was her husband, children and home. That was all. Everything. But not enough.

Maybe if he had been more like David, things would have worked out differently. If he had had lots of affairs before he was married, he could have handled Ann better. But there hadn't been many women before Ann. Since he was being honest with himself, he could tell the truth. There had only been one woman before Ann. It had been hurried and furtive in the back seat of his first car. Not what you would call experience.

It had worked out though for Ann and him. They had been in love or thought they were, which is the same thing and gradually they had become skilful lovers. Maybe Ann sometimes wondered what it would be like with someone else. After all, he did himself. But you didn't let it go any further. You stifled the thought. It was disloyal, the beginning of the break-up of a marriage. Which is why he was still haunted by Ann's leaving him so abruptly. She had started to act strangely after the Birkett party. He hadn't accompanied her and she had come home late. Very late. At least two hours after the party had finished.

No, it couldn't be another man. He shrugged the thought away irritably. If there were another man, she would not have taken the children and gone to live with her parents in the country. Right? Right. He picked up his cigarettes and lighter and left the house.

It was six by the time he returned. He had run into Mike Barker. They only had a nodding acquaintance but Ann was friendly with Delia as the children went to the same school. Delia was visiting her parents with the children and Mike had greeted him in the pub as though he were the only other man alive. They had gone back to Barker's to take what he called pot luck, which had turned out to be a superb casserole left by Delia. It had been all right for an hour or two but then the conversation had got round to Ann. Another bottle of wine was opened and Mike was getting red in the face, suggesting they took advantage of their respective wives' absence and went on the town. If words could wink, Mike's would have. Brian made an excuse and left.

No, he thought, pouring himself a drink, I am not going to

be something I'm not. I do not want to stand in bars and visit strip clubs and pretend I'm enjoying myself just because I'm not alone. I may not have made a success of my marriage but I will not make a failure of my separation.

The telephone rang. He stared at it as though it were a Martian who had just landed and was now trying to communicate in a foreign tongue. Strange how seldom it rang now Ann was no longer here. It went on ringing. He lifted the receiver.

"Brian".

"Good lord, Mother. It's you. Where are you?"

"In Bermuda still but not for long."

"But why? What's happened? Are you ill?"

"No, Brian. I'm not ill. I'm perfectly well. So well in fact that I'm coming home tonight."

"But Mother, you're supposed to stay another month. The doctor said."

"And I say," she interrupted, "that I'm coming home. I'm arriving tomorrow and I would like one of my sons to meet me."

"But of course . . ."

"I phoned the house but Edward doesn't appear to be at home. I decided not to call David since I do not wish to entrust myself to his car."

"I'll meet you, Mother."

"Good. Thank you, darling. I'll see you tomorrow. Oh . . . and Brian?"

"Yes?"

"Let Edward and David know I'm arriving, would you?"

"Yes, but . . ."

"Goodbye Brian. I'll see you tomorrow."

There was a click at the end of the line and she had gone. Brian stared at the receiver in his hand. Normal relations with the outside world had been re-established. He was alone again. He put it down slowly.

Now what was Mother cooking up this time? He'd better ring Edward.

An hour later, he had rung both his brothers several times. Neither answered.

CHAPTER THREE

The following morning Brian arrived early at the office. There was no sign of Edward's car outside and, when he looked into his office, no Edward either. It was the first time since Brian had started in the family business that Edward had not been there first, fretting and fussing and declaring that the way to earn the respect of the men was to be at work at the same time they were.

With Jennifer? No, of course, her car was outside and he did not think they would have spent the night together. He didn't think they were having an affair somehow. Not a physical affair. It would be difficult with Barbara at home and he couldn't see Jennifer in his mother's house. It was high time Edward took a place of his own. Not that his own experience of living alone was any recommendation for the state, he reflected wryly.

He looked into the board room. David was sitting reading a newspaper and stirring his coffee.

"Seen Edward?"

"Not yet. There's supposed to be a board meeting, you know. Where is everybody?" David was aggrieved. He had left a very beautiful girl in a very comfortable bed in unseemly haste in order to arrive on time and avoid Edward's scathing tongue.

"I can tell you where one person is."

"Who?" David was not particularly interested.

"Mother. She's in a plane due to touch down in an hour. I've promised to pick her up."

"Mother! Good God, what's she doing back so soon?"

"I don't know." Brian shrugged. "Anyway, the point is – does Edward know she's coming yet? I wouldn't want to get to the airport and find he's there too."

"Edward miss a board meeting? Hardly. Have you checked with Jennifer?"

"I'll do that."

Jennifer was on the phone. She waved to him to sit down. He glanced at his watch and remained standing. Seconds ticked by as she asked questions about rates and discounts, subjects which would normally interest him. At this moment, his mind was on other things. At last she put down the receiver.

"Did Edward say he was going to be late in?"

Jennifer looked at him. "Good morning Brian. No he didn't. Perhaps he overslept."

"Edward? He's never slept late in his life. Was he at home yesterday, do you know?"

Jennifer knew very well where Edward had been the previous day but she hesitated before answering. A woman who had been singled out by fate to love both the husband and eldest son of Mary Hammond and be loved by them in return, she had had long years of practice of discretion – some might say deceit – of keeping her private and professional lives, irrevocably enmeshed as they had been for twenty years and now were again, entirely separate. Of course Edward's brothers knew they saw each other out of office hours but the relationship was never discussed within them. She wondered what made Brian, the most reserved and self-effacing of the Hammonds, ask such a blunt question.

"We drove to the country for the day," she said in a neutral voice. "Why do you ask?"

In a split second, Brian realised it was not for him to tell her why. "Oh, nothing," he said. "I wondered about the board meeting."

Marion, the secretary, came in with a cup of coffee for Jennifer. "Mr. Edward just phoned," she announced. "The board meeting will start in half an hour."

"Thanks." Brian turned and fled.

Jennifer stared after him. Now what on earth was going on?

Edward Hammond was sitting in the office of Cassell, the family solicitor, puffing on one of the small, black cigars he habitually smoked. Although Cassell had had to keep him waiting, he was contented enough, thinking of the pleasant weekend he had spent, looking forward to the board meeting and getting down to business. Sunday now really set him up for the week. Dear Jenny. He patted his pocket and reassured himself the package was still there.

Cassell put down the phone at last. "I'm so sorry, Mr. Hammond, but that had to be dealt with immediately."

"All right." Edward waved away the apologies. "Can we get on now." It was a statement not a question.

Cassell opened the folder in front of him. "You and I being the Trustees, we have to deal with several items under your late father's will. . . . The first concerns a query in relation to the Estate Duty already paid."

This was quickly dealt with. Almost too quickly for Cassell's liking. He was loath to embark on the next item. He remembered all too clearly the reading of Robert Hammond's will and the venom and hatred with which Edward had reacted to it. He cleared his throat and wished he smoked. A cigarette would be a useful crutch at a time like this.

"Finally, Mr. Hammond, under Clause Three of your father's will."

"I remember it," Edward said brusquely.

Cassell coughed again. It was to be worse than he had feared. He picked up the paper and read. "Clause Three. I bequeath the sum of one thousand pounds to my daughter Barbara Kingsley for her absolute use and benefit free of all duties. Which she receives on her coming of age, of course. . . ."

"And today's her eighteenth birthday," Edward broke in, unexpectedly. "I know."

"Oh?" Cassell was amazed. Did Edward's resentment take the form of a careful watch on each movement of the Kingsleys? The answer amazed him even more.

"Her mother mentioned it."

"I see." Cassell didn't see at all. "I've arranged that Miss Kingsley, Miss Barbara Kingsley that is, will come in later this morning."

"Shall I sign the cheque?" asked Edward, anticipating him.

Cassell had already signed it. Now he passed it to Edward who scribbled his signature and handed it back. The business was concluded. Cassell put the folder away.

"How is your mother keeping?" he enquired after Edward had refused coffee.

"She's much better. The rest is doing her good as long as she avoids stress and worry."

"Quite, quite," said Cassell. "And when does she return?"

"Another month. Perhaps more." Edward got up to leave. The social niceties had been completed.

Cassell stopped him. He had known Robert Hammond for

many years. He had watched him build up the business to what it was today. He had admired and respected him. He had tried, without success, to advise him not to make Jennifer Kingsley a director. The emotional factors against were, he had felt, overwhelming. They might split the firm. Destroy the family. A private settlement could be made on Miss Kingsley and her daughter. Robert Hammand had refused. Cassell still wondered why and with the curiosity of any normal human being, he wanted to know how it was working out.

"I've always taken a great interest in the firm," he began. "I can say now that I was somewhat apprehensive about the future when your father died. Personally, I felt you had some right to be left a controlling interest but your father was adamant."

"We've managed."

Cassell ignored the message implicit in Edward's tone of voice, and continued. "The provision in your father's will that Miss Jennifer Kingsley should be a director was the one I was privately most concerned about. In view of the, shall we say, difficult emotional factors involved."

"She's good at her job. It's worked out all right." Edward stubbed out his cigar.

Cassell persisted. "So relations between yourself and Miss Kingsley are now reasonably cordial?"

For a moment Edward had a vision of Jenny with the sun shining on her hair, laughing up into his face. "Yes," he said. "You could say that."

"Good," said Cassell. "I'm glad. For the sake of the firm."

Edward arrived at the depot a minute before the revised board meeting was due to begin. He noted the absence of Brian's car and went straight to the board room. David was drinking his third cup of coffee and halfway through the crossword puzzle.

"Where's Brian?"

"Gone to the airport."

"Doesn't he know there's a board meeting?"

"Yes, but he had to meet someone."

"Meet someone . . ." Edward was furious.

"Yes. Mother." It was a minor triumph. Edward's jaw dropped.

"Mother?"

"Yes. She's decided she feels better and wants to come home."

"I see." Edward had an uneasy suspicion something was wrong. "Well, look Dave, don't mention this to Jenny . . ."

"Jenny!" He stood up as she came into the room. "Good morning. I had to talk to Cassell this morning. About you know what."

Jennifer smiled at him. Edward half-smiled then looked away.

"Where's Brian?" she asked. "Shall I go and fetch him?"

"Brian sends his apologies," said David.

"I'll explain later," said Edward in reply to Jenny's raised eyebrows. "Come on. Minutes of the previous meeting."

Jennifer didn't miss the look he exchanged with David. It made her feel vaguely uneasy. Still, she would find out the cause later. She and Edward always lunched on Monday. When they left each other on Sundays, they felt that sadness lovers feel when they have been happy together and had decided they would give themselves something to look forward to the following day.

The telephone interrupted her reverie.

"I said no calls were to be put through." Edward got up angrily.

Brian was sitting in his mother's living room, enjoying her excellent sherry and inwardly dismayed as she talked in turn to her eldest and youngest sons. She had already phoned Mrs. Wheeler, her daily help cum cook, and asked her to shop and cook for a dinner party that evening. She was now in the process of arranging that dinner party.

Mary was not pleased by Edward's reaction to her invitation. She was frankly displeased and a past mistress at making her displeasure evident.

"It's my first evening at home, Edward," she was saying. "I'm sure you could rearrange your other commitment . . . whatever it is." There was a pause as she listened to Edward. The muscles at the side of her mouth twitched. "No, Edward, I do not want you to 'look in for a drink'. I seem to have been away for a long time and I'd like to have my family around me for a few hours. I don't think that's unreasonable, do you?"

There was another pause.

"I'd rather you didn't tell me your reason, Edward," Mary said in a tired voice. "I've invited my sons to join me for dinner tonight and I hope you'll be able to come. I've missed you all very much. You must know that. And I'd like you to be here with the rest of us but you must make up your own mind. Now, may I speak to David?"

While she spoke with David, apparently with more success, Brian reflected on how Edward would make up his mind. It was evident he was planning to see Jennifer that evening. Brian shrugged. It was no concern of his. Let the best woman win.

Mary put down the phone at last.

"How's Ann?" she asked.

"Well."

"Do you see much of her?"

"When I visit the children."

"Have they been told?"

"Ann said she'd deal with that in her own time. Presumably when we've decided whether it's to be a divorce. Or what . . ."

"Yes. Well, at least divorce is honest and above-board. No one is being deceived for years on end."

Brian knew his mother was referring to herself. He changed the subject slightly.

"We've more or less decided to put the children into boarding school." His mother frowned at the thought. He tried to persuade her although it was Ann's idea not his. "It might be better for them. Get them away from all the emotional tensions."

"But can you afford it?"

That was Brian's worry too. "I'll manage somehow."

"Ann could get a job. That would help."

"Yes, I suggested it. She said she'd think about it."

"Is she still with her parents?"

"Yes. There's plenty of room there."

"Mmm," Mary looked thoughtful. "Just the same that sounds like a very temporary arrangement to me. As if she hadn't quite decided."

"Yes, I know, Mother. I managed to work that out for myself."

"Do you want her back?"

Brian tried to be honest with his mother. With himself. "I've had a pretty bad time to tell the truth. At first, I couldn't seem to concentrate on anything. I'd find myself lying on the settee, staring up at the ceiling, going over it all. The things we'd said and done. The things we hadn't said and done. At work I was making mistakes. Nothing serious, but mistakes."

"And now?" His mother probed gently.

"I'm not used to being alone. I can't say that I like it much."

"Is it Ann you miss? Or do you simply dislike a vacuum?"

"It's hard to say. Ann going, created the vacuum. I don't know."

"Make sure you do know before you do decide, one way or the other. Form without substance is much over-rated, especially in marriage."

Brian stared at his mother. He would never have expected a remark like that from her. Not with her upbringing. Not the way she had brought up her family. "You surprise me, Mother. Do you know that?"

Mary smiled. "I surprise myself quite often these days. Now let's have some lunch if you have the time and you can tell me all the other news. How is Edward? What's he been doing with himself?"

Edward toyed with his pudding. The last months with Jennifer while his mother had been abroad had transformed his life. He was still a compulsive worker. The business came first. But now he knew what it was like to have something and someone to look forward to at the end of the day. Barbara had accepted him totally. When the three of them went out together, he felt like a family. He liked the feeling.

He had been living in a fool's paradise. The absence of his mother after that second heart attack had made it all so easy. Now she was back and choices had to be made. Someone was going to be hurt. He was going to be hurt. He tried to take the easy way out. He took the package from his pocket and placed it on the table. It lay there between them.

Jennifer had felt uneasy throughout lunch. The atmosphere had been strained. She looked at the package. "What's that?"

"Would you give this to Barbara? It's her birthday present. I hope she likes it but if not they'll change it."

"You'll be seeing her tonight. You can give it to her then." Jennifer pushed it back towards him.

Edward swallowed. "I've been thinking. . . . Why don't I give her a birthday dinner. The three of us. Next weekend perhaps . . . somewhere nice, champagne, the lot."

"I expect she'll like that."

Edward was emboldened. "At a birthday party, she wants youngsters her own age, not people like me."

"She invited you."

"Yes, I know, but she was probably just being polite."

Jennifer was beginning to sense there was something deeper underlying all this. "She wasn't. And I'm sure she'd rather you gave her your present yourself."

Edward was feeling distinctly unhappy. He knew now that he wasn't going to be able to get out of this easily.

"I can't be at the party," he blurted out. "Something's cropped up."

"What?"

"It's not important but I can't get out of it. Mother's here and she's arranged a dinner-party, a sort of homecoming."

"Did you know she was coming home?" Jennifer felt numb. She remembered her last meeting with Mary Hammond.

"Not until this morning. She phoned yesterday apparently but Brian was the only one in."

"Rather short notice for dinner, isn't it? I mean, you can't be expected to be there, can you." It was an ultimatum not a question.

"Brian and David are going. I can't very well refuse."

"Why not?"

"I can't, Jennifer. I tried but she was obviously going to work herself into a state about it and it's just not worth it."

"And you don't think it's important?"

Edward tried and failed. "Well it's only one evening."

"I'm sorry," said Jennifer. "But I think it's very important indeed."

"It's just a family gathering, that's all."

Jennifer, unlike any of Mary's sons, now realised the significance of Mary Hammond's arrival.

"Did you mention me at all when you wrote to her?" she asked.

"Yes. Several times."

"What did you say?"

"All sorts of things," Edward said eagerly, trying to appease her. "About how valuable you were on the board, about adjusting to life as it is, forgetting the past. That sort of thing."

"Did you ever tell her that we've talked about getting married?"

Edward lit a cigar. He looked at Jennifer. She stared back at him coolly, waiting for an answer.

"Not in so many words. I wanted to lead up to it gradually, get her into the right frame of mind. We've got to give her time."

"How much time do you think we've got to give?"

Edward tapped his cigar on the ashtray. Jennifer made patterns with her spoon in the ice-cream. At this moment they were totally isolated, far apart as only people who are very close can be.

"I know her," Edward said doggedly. "It's got to be handled carefully."

"And while you're being so tactful and careful and considerate of her feelings, what do you think she's doing?"

"She's not doing anything."

Jennifer felt a latent violence rising within her. She could have hit Edward. "What did you say in your last letter?" she snapped.

Edward thought for a moment. "Not much. I told her about the new piece of land we're buying. Said I was thinking of taking a holiday. Oh, and I mentioned that Barbara would be eighteen today. That's all."

"That's all." That was it. Jennifer understood everything now. "Did you happen to mention that Barbara was having a party?"

"Yes I did."

"So, suddenly she changes all her plans, flies back at a day's notice, insists that you go to dinner and you don't see any connection?"

"If you're implying it's all deliberate . . ." Edward was flummoxed.

"Of course it's deliberate." Jennifer had never been more certain of anything.

"Go to all that trouble just to stop me going to Barbara's

birthday party?" Edward found the idea risible. "She wouldn't do a thing like that."

"Not just to stop you," Jennifer responded. "But to prove she can. As long as she can twist you round her little finger, she knows that she's safe."

Edward was exasperated. His masculinity was in question. "She's not twisting me. Brian and David are going so I've got to as well."

"All right. You've made your decision." Jennifer pushed her plate away. She lit a cigarette, not waiting for Edward to light it for her. Edward was at a loss. He really did not understand women. He thought Jenny would understand. He tried to take her hand. She moved it away.

"I don't want to upset her on her first day back, that's all."

Jennifer didn't answer.

"If you weren't being completely unreasonable." At the next table the couple were watching with undisguised interest. Edward almost whispered. "It's really not important, Jenny."

"You'd better decide where your priorities lie."

"I've explained it all as quietly and rationally as I can. If you won't even listen. . . ."

"I don't think much of our future prospects if you go running every time she snaps her fingers." Jennifer stubbed out her cigarette.

Edward looked at her. He felt irritable and totally at a loss. "What's happening to us?" he asked.

"Exactly what your mother intended." She glanced at her watch. "It's late. Can you get the bill, please?"

Edward tried again. "Don't make a big deal out of it, Jenny, please. Try to be sensible. See my point of view."

Jennifer was infuriatingly calm. "I'll tell Barbara you're not coming."

"I'll make it up to her another time."

Jennifer knew that you can never make anything up to anyone at any time. She went straight to the point. "Your mother said you'd never marry me while she was alive."

"She was distraught. It was just something to say."

"She knew you better than I did." Jennifer's voice was icy. If he hadn't loved her, he would have hated her at that moment.

"Be reasonable," he begged.

"We know where we stand now." She signalled to the waiter. "And perhaps it's just as well – before things went too far."

CHAPTER FOUR

Edward's misery and guilt crystallised into anger when he turned into the depot to see Bill Riley chatting with a stranger. The stranger handed Riley a card, shook hands, got into a large saloon car and drove past him with a casual wave of the hand.

Edward stormed over to Riley. "Who the hell is that?"

Riley looked at him. He had worked for Hammonds all his life. He had known Edward as a boy. He was not impressed by his blustering. He looked at the card in his hand then passed it to Edward.

"Name's Carter. He wanted me to show him round the new land."

"What for? Don't you have any work to do that you can traipse around on sight-seeing tours? You'll be selling bloody souvenirs next!"

Riley turned away. "Well, I'd best be getting on."

Edward stormed up the stairway and into his office. David was waiting for him. He tossed the card over to him. "Read that."

David read it. "Carter Express Ltd."

"I've heard of him," said Edward. "He's an Australian. Runs a tinpot express parcel and distribution firm in Southwark and now he's trying to con his way into our backyard. Get Brian here. And Jennifer."

Twenty minutes later, Brian had broken several traffic laws and was in the board-room. Jennifer, however, was under a hairdryer and could not be summoned. Although he railed at her absence, Edward was secretly pleased. Now he could storm and rage at her and assuage his own feelings of guilt towards her.

"Right," he began. "I found this merchant Carter ferreting around our new land today."

"It's not ours yet," said Brian mildly.

"We made an offer and they accepted it."

"Subject to raising the necessary money," Brian pointed out.

"You've done that."

"I'm dealing with it, Ted. But it's not finalised yet."

There was silence for a moment. This was news to Edward and David. They were stunned. Brian looked at them both. They didn't look back. He felt hunted suddenly, aware he was in the wrong.

"You've had plenty of time, Brian." Edward was speaking quietly for once. This was too important for a shouting match.

"I've had a lot to do . . . I've been working on it . . . looking for the best terms . . ." Brian's voice tailed off.

"Let's get this straight," said Edward. "Are you telling us that as far as the agents are concerned, it's not settled?"

"They know the position," Brian admitted.

"But they could consider other offers?"

"They could, yes . . ."

"Ring them."

Brian looked at David but there was no help forthcoming from him. He was as disturbed as Edward.

"Ring the agents." Edward was relentless.

Brian looked at his watch. "It's getting late."

"Try."

Brian always found it embarrassing to talk business on the telephone in Edward's presence. He toyed with the idea of going to his own office. Edward nodded at the phone on his desk. Brian lifted the receiver and dialled. He was sorry when it answered.

"Hullo. It's Brian Hammond. Is Mr. Green there, please? . . . All right, I'll speak to Mr. Patterson." There was a pause. "Hullo, Mr. Patterson? It's about that land. . . . Yes. . . . Yes. . . . How good? . . . Yes, I see. Hold on a minute, will you, please." He covered the mouthpiece and addressed Edward. "They received a firm offer late this afternoon."

"Who from? Carter?"

"I don't know."

"Stall it."

Brian spoke into the telephone again. "Hullo, Mr. Patterson. Has that offer been put up to the owners yet? No. Well, would you ask Mr. Green to call me first thing in the morning before he does anything about it? . . . Yes, I'm sorry about the delay but we are still interested. Very interested. Yes. Thanks very much." He hung up.

"We need that land," said David, breaking the silence. "We could be strangled for lack of space without that land."

"I'm sorry," said Brian, "I had no reason to think there'd be any difficulty."

Edward snapped into being Managing Director and Chairman of the board. "You'd better go to your office, Brian, and get on the telephone to your financial friends. Get them at home, get them out of the bath if you have to but make sure we've got that money by tomorrow morning."

Brian hesitated. If only it were so simple. "I'm afraid the position's more difficult," he said. "This afternoon's offer was superior to ours."

"How much superior?"

"Patterson wouldn't say. But he implied it was considerably higher."

"Can we afford to go up any more?"

"I don't know. I'll do what I can." Brian got up and left. He looked very unhappy. David felt sorry for him. He knew what it was like to be in Edward's bad books. He tried to defend him.

"He's let everything get him down."

"He's let everything get on top of him. If that new land's cut off, we're in trouble. Big trouble. There'll be an emergency board meeting tomorrow at noon."

Barbara Kingsley was at home. The kitchen was full of food. Glasses and wine were ready. Her hair was pinned up in rollers and *it* had pride of place on the mantelpiece among all the birthday cards. *It* was a cheque. The cheque. The cheque for one thousand pounds which her father had left her. It was her passport to freedom. Now she could do what she liked. The telephone rang as she was admiring the beautiful noughts.

"Hello. Oh hello, Mrs. Hammond. I thought you were abroad?"

"Oh?" Mary Hammond was fond of Barbara but she could not resist indulging her quest for information. "I expect your mother told you that?"

"Yes," said Barbara with the innocence of youth. She didn't share her mother's distrust of Mary Hammond. She felt she had had a rough deal, deceived by her husband – Barbara's father – for so many years. "I heard Edward telling her."

So they were still seeing each other. Information acquired, Mary changed tack. "Well Barbara, I just telephoned to congratulate you on your coming of age."

"Thank you." Barbara was touched.

"I only arrived back today," Mary went on. "I couldn't send you a card but there's a little present I want to give you." She interrupted Barbara's protests. "I've always told you there's no reason why we can't be good friends, you and I, and I hope you'll try to meet me halfway . . ."

"Well, thank you. Thanks a lot, Mrs. Hammond."

"Now. Did you get your cheque today?"

"Oh yes," Barbara was bubbling over. "Mr. Cassell wanted to invest it for me. Said I could earn a pound a week from it." She laughed at the memory of the solicitor's solemn face. "But I told him I wanted the money to go to art school. For equipment. And travel. And everything . . ."

"And you're still planning to move into a flat of your own?"

"Yes. Yes, I think so."

"You must have a lot to get on with. I'll ring off now, Barbara. Happy birthday."

The phone clicked. The door slammed. Jennifer was home.

"Who was that?"

"Mrs. Hammond. She wanted to wish me happy birthday. And she says she's a present for me."

"Oh." Jennifer checked her suspicions. She must not spoil this evening for Barbara just because it had been spoiled for her. "That reminds me. Edward asked me to give you this." She handed over the package.

"I already had your present," Barbara looked at her mother.

"This is from Edward."

"Do you know what it is?"

"No."

Barbara frowned then started to smile as she opened the wrappings and discovered the exquisite silver bracelet. "Hey, look at this."

"He said you could change it if you didn't like it."

"I love it." Barbara slipped it over her wrist. "Why didn't he bring it himself?"

"He's not coming."

"Why not?"

"He's having dinner with his mother." Jennifer lit a cigarette. Barbara considered her.

"Couldn't he come later?"

"I don't know. I didn't ask him."

"Why not?"

"Barbara, must you ask one question after another?"

"Only if I don't get an answer the first time."

"He felt that he wasn't able to come and that's all there is to say about it."

"He could have phoned me. It is supposed to be my party."

Jennifer looked at her daughter. "And it's going to be a good one," she said gently. "The first guests will be here soon. Why don't you and I have a drink to get into the mood?"

"Great. I'll get the wine. White?"

Jennifer nodded.

Barbara came back with the bottle and poured the drinks. She handed a glass to Jennifer. Jennifer raised it to her. "Happy birthday, darling."

David sipped his drink. He had been deputed by his two brothers to leave the office early and join his mother. She certainly looked well. She smiled at him.

"Well now, tell me all your news." The guaranteed conversation-stopper.

"Nothing much seems to have happened." David groped his memory. "I bought a new suit. I'm thinking of changing my car." He had a brainwave. "I've been working very hard mainly."

"Well, how about work?"

David thought of the scene in the office he had just left. "I still don't like getting up early," he answered. "I don't think I'll ever get used to it. But, on the whole, fine. Edward seems to take my presence for granted now so on the whole I suppose you could say I've arrived."

"Good." Mary smiled at him. Mothers always have a particularly soft spot for their last-born.

"I'm enjoying it to tell the truth. They've kept me in charge of sales and new business and I think I earn my director's fees. But I'm also taking more of a hand in the actual running of the business and I like that. It's a sort of daily challenge."

"So you're quite the successful young business man?" Mary

remembered him pink and newly-bathed, asking why he couldn't stay up late like Brian.

"I know. It's ghastly, isn't it?"

"I think it's splendid. I'm sure you didn't expect to go on doing nothing all your life. . . . And who's your latest girl friend? she added casually.

"No one special. I adore all women," David said lightly.

"Don't make fun. I'm serious. I'd like to see you married and settled down, before I . . ." she faltered. "I feel perfectly all right now but it could easily happen again. . . ."

"Oh come on, Mother. You'll live forever." David hated the turn the conversation was taking.

"No I shan't." Mary gazed at the clock on the mantelpiece. "It doesn't seem long ago that I had a husband I trusted, three sons, one of them married, grandchildren . . . and now . . . now my husband is dead and I know that for the last twenty years of his life he had another woman. Brian's marriage . . . if that breaks down, I shall lose my grandchildren. They'll stay with Ann. Edward . . . Edward seems very confused. Is it any wonder that I'd like you to meet some nice girl?"

"That's my problem, Mother. I never meet any nice girls." David grinned. She looked at him and saw him at thirteen, school tie askew, grinning at her and explaining away his latest school report.

"You're impossible and I shall stop wasting my breath."

"And I'll have another drink." David got up.

Mary didn't give up so easily. "Think about what I've said, David."

David fiddled with the ice-bucket and hoped Brian and Edward would get here soon.

Brian did arrive shortly afterwards. Two down, one to go, David thought as he got up for yet another round of drinks. What was worse than making polite conversation with your own family? Nothing, he decided. Mary sipped her drink and wondered whether Edward would show up. She had felt confident he would this afternoon. Perhaps she had overestimated herself? Underestimated Jennifer?

Edward at that moment was drinking a large whisky with an attractive woman. If Mary had seen them together, she would have been pleased. The woman was not Jennifer Kingsley.

What strange stroke of chance had made Nancy Lincoln telephone him that very morning? Edward crumpled the piece of paper with her telephone number in his pocket. When she had called that morning and left a message, his first reaction had been to throw it away. That evening, after the disastrous scene with Jennifer and the appalling revelation that the land was not yet theirs, the last thing he felt like was going home. But go home he must. Eventually. First he would have a drink. In the office? No. A pub? He rejected the idea. And then he remembered. The slip of paper was in the waste-basket. He fished it out. Called the number and here he was. Nancy was as warm and comforting as ever. He smiled at her.

"One more," he handed her his glass. "Then I must go home. Family celebration."

Mary felt nothing but relief as she heard the front door slam. Edward. She had won. She went to greet him.

"Sorry I'm late. Things cropped up."

"At least you're here now." She patted the seat beside her. "We're all together again."

All three of her sons smiled at her and looked away, each lost in his own thoughts. Brian looked very unhappy. His mind was on money. The thought of the board meeting the next day loomed large.

"Let's all forget our troubles for one night," Mary said. "Make this a happy occasion."

He was being a brute. Brian tried. "Yes, Mother. Let's do that."

"I can't tell you how good it feels to be home again and have my family around me, the way it used to be in the old days."

Edward couldn't take this. "The old days are in the past, Mother."

Mary was not to be budged. "But we still want to be together. We're still a family. And that is important," she insisted.

The family looked distinctly uneasy. Mary got to her feet. She had had a few drinks and she was feeling sentimental and bold. She was determined to make her point. Edward got to his feet too.

"Is dinner ready?" he asked.

"No. I want you all to join me in a toast," she replied.

Brian and David got to their feet, a little embarrassed, wondering what was coming next.

Mary raised her glass. "The family," she said.

They had to go along with it but none of her sons could bring himself to repeat the words. One by one, they drank.

Brian took a small sip.

Then David.

Edward looked at his glass. It was almost full. He swallowed it down in one.

CHAPTER FIVE

The family. Mary Hammond sipped her breakfast coffee and thought about them. The dinner had been quite a success and had ended late. The boys had avoided talking business although she had tried to bring the conversation round that way several times. She had an uneasy suspicion that something was wrong and it was Brian's fault. He had been very quiet. On the other hand, that might be because he was still worrying about Ann.

No, she didn't think it could be. He had been very frank with her about his feelings. It no longer seemed to be loneliness for Ann in particular but the general loneliness. It was funny how men went to pieces in these situations. Women were stronger really. They seemed to have more inner resources to cope with life alone. Then again, they had to. She had had years alone. When the children were babies asleep upstairs while she sat and waited for Robert to come home. Then Edward had joined his father at work and David had gone to boarding school and university. Somehow, a woman managed to fill the long hours. Perhaps it was best that Robert had died first. He would never have coped either. Except, of course, he would have been free to marry Jennifer Kingsley.

Jennifer Kingsley. Edward had arrived very late for dinner last night. Had he been with her first? She had not dared to ask. It was tacitly understood that her name was not mentioned in this house in anything other than a professional connection. But she would like to know. She was back now and fighting fit.

Well, to work. She put the breakfast things on a tray ready for Mrs. Wheeler to carry out. She was going to the shops today. She had to take Edward's suit to the cleaner. It was hanging in the hall cupboard. She took it out and methodically went through the pockets. She removed a box of matches and a handkerchief from the trouser pocket and laid them on the hall table. There was nothing in the jacket except a small scrap of paper. She took it out and smoothed it. There was a telephone number and a name. Mary stared at it for a moment then picked up the telephone and dialled.

It rang three times.

"Hullo. Yes. This is Nancy Lincoln. Who's that?"

"Oh," Mary hesitated. "I'm not sure if I have the right number. Is that Mrs. Lincoln of South Lane?"

"No, I'm afraid not. This is Burley Mansions."

"I seem to have made a terrible mistake. I'm sorry to have bothered you." Mary rang off. The voice was promising. She sounded young and attractive. Of course that could be misleading. She might be a business acquaintance. And Edward might not be interested in her anyway. She picked up the telephone again.

Barbara answered the telephone immediately. Her party had been a great success. They had danced and talked till two in the morning but she had been up at eight to have breakfast with her mother. Jennifer had looked very tired.

"Hullo, Barbara. Did you have a pleasant birthday?"

"Oh marvellous, Mrs. Hammond."

"And was the party a success?"

"Great. It was a pity Edward missed it."

So Edward had not been there. Good. Mary beamed down the receiver at Barbara.

"Barbara dear, I'm going out shopping now and I want to bring you my gift. Would it be all right if I dropped it off in say an hour?"

"Oh, but you needn't. It would be a nuisance."

"Not at all, Barbara. It's something I particularly want you to have."

"Then that would be great."

"My pleasure." Mary put down the phone. She had just one more phone call to make.

Jennifer answered the telephone immediately. She felt old, old, old, this morning. Barbara had looked so pretty and carefree last night. And so grown-up. She was the mother of a young adult who would soon be leaving home to lead her own life. And what sort of life would she have then? Mary Hammond was the last person she wanted to speak to.

"Miss Kingsley, I felt I must telephone. I've just spoken to Barbara and I wanted to give her a small birthday gift but I realise I should have asked you first."

"Well, it's up to Barbara," Jennifer said curtly. "She's grown up now."

"I hope you know that I have a considerable affection for

her. Whatever took place in the past is nothing to do with Barbara."

"Look, do you think we could talk another time," Jennifer interrupted. "I've a lot of work. . . ."

"There was one other thing, Miss Kingsley." Mary Hammond was unassailable when she wanted to do something. "When I was abroad, I did a great deal of thinking and I realised that, whatever I may feel, my late husband really wasn't very fair to you either. However, Edward is more straightforward so I presume he's told you about his new association. I must be frank and tell you that I hope it will work out."

Mary put down the phone. Now she knew how sportsmen felt when they won. She was elated.

Jennifer felt sick. It was strange. Her mind did not function for a moment. She just felt physically sick. Words from Mary's remarks finally started to hammer at her brain. "My late husband." Mary always made a point of referring to "my husband" in front of Jennifer. "Miss Kingsley." She always emphasised the Miss. And what was it she had said about Edward? So straightforward. And what was this association? What had Edward done last night? Had he had dinner with his mother?

"How was Barbara's party?" Edward stood by her desk. It was as though she had conjured him up. She looked at him curiously detached. He looked the same. He was smiling at her.

"Fine."

"How about lunch?"

"No. I've a lot of work."

"Dinner then. I'll book a table."

"I'm having an early night. You probably need one too."

"What do you mean?" He looked so innocent, she was tempted to say no more, to accept his invitation. This was the man she wanted to spend the rest of her life with. But she had to be able to live with herself. She could not accept less than the best. Not this time.

"What did you do last night?" she asked.

"Worked. Had a few drinks afterwards."

"Who with?"

Edward stared at her. He loved Jenny but he had an old-fashioned view of women. They didn't ask questions like that. "Why?" he asked.

"Is it a secret?"

"No. I was with an old friend."

"Whom you'd prefer to remain anonymous?" she challenged him.

"Someone called Nancy Lincoln. You don't know her. Why the interrogation?"

"You never mentioned this old friend before."

"We're not a pair of kids, Jenny. We've both had previous relationships. I'm not a monk. But it ended. As soon as I knew how I felt about you."

"And last night?"

"I asked you to see me but you wouldn't."

"So you pick up where you left off elsewhere."

They looked at each other, assessing each other, totally detached from each other. Edward did not know what to say. How could he explain how he had felt yesterday. The feeling of guilt, of being torn between two women and not knowing which to choose. The blessed escape to a third woman who asked no questions, expected nothing from him but that he be there? It was Jennifer who spoke. Her voice was cold.

"I shared a man before, Edward. Because he was married and had a family, even though he wanted to get a divorce and marry me, I wouldn't let him. That all started when I was young but I'm not young any more and I'll tell you this. I'm never going to share a man again. So don't talk to me about love any more because I don't believe you and I never will."

Edward stared at her. He had no intention of talking about love. At that moment, he almost hated her. He felt harassed and nagged. He found himself in the wrong and he wasn't quite sure why. If he could have spoken in that moment, found the right words, all might have been well. But Edward was not an articulate lover. He left without saying anything.

CHAPTER SIX

The board meeting had been going on for over an hour. The family were on one side; Jennifer was on the other. At least that was how it felt. There had been a lot of talk but very few decisions. Jennifer could hardly bear to look at Edward sitting in the chair, so remote. He looked hard, withdrawn. David and Brian were doing most of the talking.

Perhaps family businesses were a bad thing, she thought. A contradiction in terms. Certainly David was acting most un-brotherly towards Brian. The thought of the new land being lost to them was almost more than he could bear.

"We've got to have that land," he shouted.

"It's no use your keeping on saying we've got to. . . ."

"Expansion. You've always agreed about it."

Jennifer glanced at Brian. He looked defeated, old. "Within our means," she interjected.

David rounded on her. "New business generates extra traffic. The depot's bursting at the seams already. There's only the one available piece of adjoining land and without it, we come to a dead stop."

"We all know that," said Jennifer. "But now that Brian's secured the finance to match Carter's bid. . . ."

"I didn't say I had."

Jennifer stared at him. "You did. I took a note."

"Finance, yes. But from more than one source and it's expensive. We pitched our first offer high and to improve on it substantially could be a millstone that would sink us."

"We're sunk either way," said David.

"The agents are prepared to hold off for a while," explained Brian. "They say they didn't realise there'd be so much interest in that land." Jennifer seemed to be the only one listening to him sympathetically. He addressed his words to her. "Not that that's to our advantage. Let's face it. We're involved in a Dutch auction now. With Carter."

There was silence for a moment. Edward lit a cigar and leaned back.

"Right then. We'd better start being businesslike. David,

Brian, I asked you to spend the morning finding out a few things. I told you I wanted to know everything there is to know about Harry Carter and I told you I didn't care how you got your information. First I'll tell you what I found out."

They all looked at him. This was Edward at his best – tough, ruthless. It was not the Edward Jennifer liked best.

"I went to see Carter at lunchtime. I tried to persuade him to back off but he wouldn't. He wants to transfer his whole ramshackle outfit into our backyard, lock, stock and barrel. Incidentally, he also tried to steal Riley. Right, David – what did you discover?"

"I prowled around his yard. On the face of it, he runs a pretty makeshift outfit. He's got a fleet of vans which he built up from scratch. I talked to some of his men. They all like him. The mechanics know their job and the vans are in good shape and well maintained. The drivers get paid on a bonus and incentive scheme. He's doing a lot of work."

"Brian?"

Brian looked up. "Yes. His past balance sheets are very healthy."

"What about the present?"

Brian looked uneasy. He lacked Edward's working-class toughness; David's public-school deviousness. This was not his way of doing business.

"I'm not especially proud of the way I had to get some of this information," he began, as though he hoped they would stop him. "Some of it's hearsay, some of it's third hand. . . ."

"All right, all right, let's get on," said Edward.

"Carter came here from Australia ten years ago. He was married but that ended in divorce and his wife went back to Sydney."

"Was there another woman involved?" Edward's interest was purely in whether this information could be turned to advantage but Jennifer was appalled. Was this what they had come to? This seeking out of smutty secrets which could be used to destroy a person? She thought of her own life, her love for Robert Hammond. She remembered how pure, how right it had seemed until it was revealed at a meeting not unlike this. That relationship had been diminished by the so-called objective views of outsiders. She shuddered.

Brian was answering Edward. "Yes, there was another

woman. They lived together for a year but they split up. He's supposed to visit night clubs a lot now. . . ."

"Do we have to listen to this sort of thing?" Jennifer burst out.

"Yes, we do," said Edward.

"The worst kind of personal gossip?"

"Anything." Edward looked at her. "Anything that'll help us to deal with Carter. Go on, Brian."

"There's a bit of mystery about his business affairs." Edward was listening with close attention. If he felt Jenny's distress, he did not show it. "The last balance sheet lodged referred to his financial year ending nearly two years ago. There's nothing unusual about that though, as you know."

"No, no, go on." Edward was impatient.

"Profits, excellent. But personally, I wouldn't have been happy with his asset situation." He took another page of notes from the folder. "From now on, I'm relying on information from here and there, so I can't guarantee its accuracy. The business is flourishing, perhaps too flourishing. There are certain signs that he's badly overstretched, taken on too many commitments. Bills which he used to settle promptly now take two or three months to pay. He used to have a fairly large house. He sold that recently and moved into something much smaller."

"The house was probably too big for him if he was on his own," Jennifer found herself defending the unknown Carter.

"Perhaps," Brian agreed. "As I say, none of this is concrete."

"Perhaps he needed money badly," Edward put in. "Anything else?"

Brian nodded. "There are one or two people, who should never have talked to me about it of course, who wonder how he's managed to stay afloat at all. One suggested that he was using cross bank accounts. That means he keeps out of trouble by having several bank accounts, drawing on one, meeting that by writing a cheque on another, and so on."

David was triumphant. "Well then, we're in the clear. If he's got to go to these lengths, he can't afford to buy that land."

The triumph was short-lived. "There is a certain finance house. I wouldn't deal with them myself . . . but they're prepared to back him to a figure far beyond anything we could afford."

Edward was undismayed. "That's easy to fix. A quiet word to the wise. They won't back him once they know how shaky he is."

Brian shook his head. "They won't just want the land as security. They'll want everything. They'd be quite happy to foreclose and get not only the land but Carter Express as well. As I say, this particular finance house doesn't enjoy the best of reputations."

Edward did not quite understand. "Carter's not a fool, whatever else he is. Why would he walk into a situation like that?"

"I don't know," answered Brian. "Perhaps it's the last gamble left he can take."

"It's ridiculous," Edward was livid. He had found out the worst and he wasn't able to do anything about it. "We're bigger, stronger, much more solid and yet you're telling us that he can outbid us for land we desperately need."

"It's a paradox but it's the case." Brian pushed away his notes in distaste. He had never enjoyed a job of work less.

"Then there's nothing we can do about it." Jennifer wasn't sure whether to be pleased or sorry. She was sorry about the land; pleased that the sordid information they had obtained had been to no avail.

David had been thinking. He looked up now and said, "There is something we could do. We could take him over."

There was a stunned silence. This was a new thought.

"We take him over?" said Edward. "What other brilliant ideas have you got?"

"All I'm saying," David spoke quietly. He knew it was the only way to get Edward to take him seriously and he checked his natural reaction to snap back at the implied criticism. "All I'm saying is, let's examine it. We're not really in the distribution side although we've nibbled at it under the Borret contract."

"The sooner that expires the better," Edward looked round the table for affirmation.

"It's paying now," pointed out David, "except that the warehouse isn't fully utilised yet. We can't use the Borret vans, they're fully employed. But Carter's got a fleet of vans and the business to go with it."

Brian was impressed. "There is a certain logic in combining long haul with local distribution. It's worth examining."

"Yes, yes," said Edward. "I see that. But if we can't outbid the man for a piece of land as you have told us, I think, where, can you tell me, are we supposed to find the money to buy him out? Come on, let's talk sense."

Brian was on happier territory now. This idea was appealing. "Not buy him out," he corrected Edward. "Take him over. In which case, we use paper money."

"Which we print ourselves, is that it?" Edward was heavily sarcastic.

"Yes. Shares. A block of shares."

"That's it." David was excited. The idea he'd thrown into the meeting was beginning to take form. And it was his idea.

"There'd probably have to be some further inducement for Carter," Brian added.

"You mean apart from handing him a chunk of this business on a plate?" Edward was resisting the idea for all he was worth.

"We could offer him a seat on the board."

Edward couldn't believe his ears. "Are you out of your mind?"

"It's common practice," said Brian. "It's another way of paying him, by way of director's fees and a voice in the decision-making process, in return for which he'd exercise a managerial function."

"Where do you dig up all these long words?" Edward's face was livid. "I'll tell you what all that spells, shall I. A vote. A vote at this table."

"We'd always be in the majority," said David.

"We? Who's we?" asked Edward.

"The family and Jennifer," said Brian.

"Yes," Edward smiled round at them. It was not a pleasant smile. "Well, I remember being out-voted by my family and Jennifer once and we nearly got taken over ourselves as a result."

It was beginning to get dark. David got up and switched on the light. None of them looked very happy. Jennifer was tired. She looked strained. There was an atmosphere between her and Ted which he couldn't pin down. Maybe he was imagining it. He felt pretty tired himself after last night's dinner and this morning's fact-raking session.

"It would be a way of expanding the distribution side without laying out a lot of capital," Brian went on.

David sat down. "Carter would have a guaranteed long haul carrier from us."

"There is a case to be made out for such a merging of interests," Brian was busy working out contract clauses in his head. This could save the day.

"Merging?" Edward put. "You started by talking about a take-over. Now it's turning into a merger."

"We'd be swallowing him, not the other way round," said David.

Jennifer had remained fairly silent throughout the exposition of David's plan. Now she spoke. "We're losing sight of the fact that the only reason this ever came up is because we look like losing a piece of land we need."

"And that was no act of God," said Edward, looking straight at Brian. "That was because it wasn't treated as urgently as it should have been."

"I've already apologised," said Brian. "Will another apology help?"

"It won't put it right," Edward glowered.

"Carter would withdraw his offer," David cut in cheerfully, "and the new company would buy the land at a sensible price."

"Can we be sure of that?" asked Jennifer.

"It would be in Carter's interests as well as ours," Brian answered her.

A phrase in David's last speech had jolted Edward. He went over it again in his head before speaking.

"What new company?" he enquired.

"Well, it would in effect be a new company," said David.

"Hammond and Carter Transport Services?" Edward couldn't believe it. "You want his name plastered all over a fleet of lorries he's never done a damn thing to build up? Listen, the old man put his name on this firm and that'll do me."

"The old man started it but now his sons are running it."

"We're still Hammonds," said Edward.

"Agreed," said David. "We must keep the family name to emphasise where the control lies but we should be a new animal if we took Carter over."

Jennifer was listening with growing annoyance. She did not like the idea of a change of name. "You three seem to have forgotten that the Hammond Brothers don't entirely own this business. I own a quarter of it which your father left to me and I don't remember anything in his will about changing the name."

"Right," said Edward. It was pleasant to be in accord with Jenny again if only for a moment.

"Times change, Jenny." David, the youngest, was the most flexible.

"People, too, it seems to me," answered Jenny hotly. Edward looked at her. The accord had only been for a moment. That remark had been directed at him.

Brian tried to make the peace. "I think David only meant to float the idea."

"No," said David. "I'll make a formal proposal."

"I think we've discussed the take-over pretty thoroughly," said Brian. "Provided we can negotiate favourable terms, taking over Carter's business would make good sense. A major factor being the acquisition of the land which we're at present competing for, but also as a marriage of interest. I propose the question be put."

"I'll take a vote," said Edward.

"Just a minute," Jenny blurted out. "There's more than self-interest at stake here."

"The discussion's closed. On David's proposal that we start negotiations. All those in favour."

David and Brian raised their hands.

"Against."

Jennifer did not raise her hand. "I'm dead against this," she began. "It would change the whole character of this firm. Once you start talking about take-overs, you start talking about using people for your own ends and that's not the way this business was built up."

Edward took the opportunity to hit back at Jennifer. She had hurt his feelings badly. "I don't want speeches. Just your vote."

She raised her hand. "Against."

"Well, with your casting vote, that decides it," David said sourly. He knew that Edward would be against anything that took Hammonds from a family firm into the realm of big business. Edward surprised him.

"I don't need a casting vote. I'm in favour. Carter's tried to swing a fast one on us and it'll be a pleasure to go to work on him. The motion's carried."

Jennifer got up to leave. He motioned her to remain seated.

"We haven't finished yet. David's proposal that we change the name of the firm."

"It's not an urgent matter," Brian sensed Jennifer's distress. "I think we should postpone that."

"The motion's on the table. Those in favour." He looked at David. "You proposed it."

David raised his hand reluctantly.

"And me. That makes two," said Edward. "Those against."

"Yes." Jennifer raised her hand. She wished she could smash it into Edward's face.

Brian didn't do anything. Then he looked at Jenny's face and raised his hand. "Against."

"Two in favour, two against." Edward was taunting Jennifer now. "So it's my casting vote."

"It's normal practice for the Chairman to come down on the side of the status quo," Brian pointed out.

"I don't need you to tell me what normal practice is."

"It's only fair," Brian protested. "Then the matter can be discussed again later until a genuine majority emerges."

"My casting vote goes in favour of the proposal, which is therefore carried." Edward brooked no objection. "Brian, you can start investigating the availability of an alternative company name which will make it plain that the Hammonds continue to control this business. The meeting's closed."

He got up and walked out.

David and Brian looked at Jennifer. She looked very small, shrunken. They looked at each other. They did not feel the elation they should be feeling.

"I'm sorry," David said. "That suggestion sort of got out of control. I didn't think Ted would steamroller it through like that. Do you know what's wrong with him, Brian?"

"No, I don't. Do you, Jenny?"

"Yes. Yes, I do. Excuse me." Close to tears, Jennifer got up and left the board-room.

CHAPTER SEVEN

By mutual consent, David and Brian decided that they deserved a very large, very dry martini in very plush surroundings. Half an hour later they decided they deserved a second. The bar brought back memories for Brian. He used to dine here with Ann from time to time.

"Shall we eat?" David asked him. "The menu looks pretty good."

"No, I've got to go home and do some work on this take-over idea. And Carol's schoolteacher is coming over. Still, that shouldn't take long."

"Are you in favour?"

"Of the take-over? It takes two. Carter might not like it."

"From what you were saying, he could be made to like it."

"A shotgun wedding? Well, they work sometimes."

David suddenly lost interest. The man at the next table had got up, leaving his companion in full view. It was Jill. He hadn't seen Jill since the night of the Birkett party when he had told her that from now on it was work for him with no time to play. Play there had been, of course, but Sally Woolf had been on the scene then. Sally. So clever. So sophisticated. So good in bed. Sally was a woman. Jill was a girl in comparison. But such a beautiful girl. She looked marvellous tonight. They'd had good times together in and out of bed. He walked over to the table.

"Hullo, Jill."

She seemed pleased to see him but wary. He must have hurt her quite badly.

"I haven't seen you since the Birkett party," he said.

"That was a boring occasion," she smiled at him.

"Is that fellow your boy friend?"

"Someone I go out with. He's gone to check our table." The message was obvious. Get lost. David tried the memories game.

"The food was quite good here – in our day."

"It still is." Jill got up to go.

"Are you still living at the same address?"

"No, I'm living with someone now."

"Oh."

"A girl friend," she laughed. It was good to see David Hammond at a loss. She felt she could cope with him this time. In the past, it was always he who had made the running.

"Give me your number. I'll give you a ring and we can have a drink sometime." David was the confident male again.

"You can reach me through the agency. You have the number."

"You're still modelling then?"

"Yes, David. Life goes on, doesn't it?" She smiled at him again then walked into the restaurant.

"Who was that?" Brian was appreciative. "Girl friend?"

"Ex."

"She's much too pretty to be anybody's ex."

Nancy Lincoln was looking forward to seeing Edward again. Their affair had been brief but comforting. He had arrived in her life when her marriage was finally breaking up and she had needed somebody. He had needed somebody too and for the same reasons: to have someone to meet and phone occasionally, to talk to and touch, someone who ensured you were part of the human race and not just an automaton who worked, ate and slept. She had accepted the news that there was a special somebody in Edward's life and they must therefore stop seeing each other. They were friends first. Lovers second. Anyway, her husband needed her still. She had gone back to him. Now she was alone again. Yesterday, she had needed to talk to someone. She had telephoned Edward. She was pleased when he had not answered himself. The ball was in his court. He could either ring her back or not ring her back. He had rung.

She poured two whiskies. The doorbell rang. Good old dependable Edward. He kissed her on the cheek. "Nice to see you," he said.

"Nice to see you," she replied. "Now try that once more." She clung to him hungrily. It had been a long time. Edward was taken aback for a moment. This wasn't what he had planned. It was Jennifer he loved. He just wanted whisky and sympathy. But her lips were warm. He kissed her back. Then kissed her again. It was Nancy who broke away.

"Come on. The whisky's poured."

Edward sat back comfortably. Nancy was a relaxing woman to be with. Good-looking too. Blonde, bosomy – his type.

"I'm glad I rang you," she said. "I just rang to see how you were." Every woman, however honest, cannot be totally honest at such moments. "Later I wished I hadn't. You know, after all, we had broken up and. . . ."

"I'm glad you rang."

"What happened? Did you have a row with her? Whoever she is?" Nancy smiled at him. She wasn't needling him. It was genuine interest combined with gentle teasing. Edward didn't mind at all.

"A bit more than that, I'm afraid." He swirled the liquid around his glass. "I thought it was going to work. You know, really work."

Nancy nodded. "What went wrong?"

"All sorts of things," Edward was explaining to himself as much as to Nancy. "On the face of it, because I put family obligations first. But I've been wondering if perhaps that wasn't the real reason at all. Perhaps that was just an excuse."

"An excuse on her part or yours?"

Edward was surprised. The question had not occurred to him before.

"And how about you?" he asked, not wishing to dwell on his own miseries.

"No change."

"Why don't you divorce him and be done with it?"

"I can't divorce him since I was the one who walked out on him. And he won't divorce me. Says he's still in love with me." She grimaced. "Actually, he just can't bear giving up one of his possessions. Anyway, that means I've got to wait until five years have elapsed. I shudder to think how old I shall be by then. I suppose that's his idea. Make sure that no one else wants me."

"I shouldn't think that's very likely." Edward got up and sat beside her. He wanted her very much.

Pamela Graham had been Carol's schoolteacher. Brian had met her briefly at Open Days and found her pleasant enough. She was a nice looking woman, he thought and then dismissed her. After all, Ann had been at his side on those occasions and with Ann around, very few other women commanded a man's attention. Looking at Pamela now, as she sipped her sherry, neatly dressed in skirt and sweater, he decided she was one of those women whom you probably know for some time before you realise quite how attractive they are.

"I've brought Carol's exercise books and some other things she left behind. They're in this bag." She wondered how to put what she had to say next. "I must say that I'm sorry Carol's leaving. I'll miss her. And I must say that I think she's very young to be sent away to boarding school. At her age, children are better off in the family environment."

"My wife and I aren't together."

"Oh, I see."

Brian smiled. "It's funny. People ask me how Ann is and I smile and answer and keep up this front of being together. I don't know why. I suppose I can't face all the explanations. Somehow it wasn't too hard to say it to you."

He got up and poured her another drink without asking. He was enjoying talking to this woman. He didn't want her to go yet. He wanted to know more about her. She liked music. Ann hadn't been interested so he had given up going to concerts. And her favourite composer was Mahler. Brian's favourite.

"You're probably a very good teacher," he said to her.

"Not a qualified one, I'm afraid. I taught for a few terms originally to fill in before I went to college. But I liked it and stayed on so all I can do now is stay where I am. There's nothing else I can do." She crossed her legs. She had nice legs, he noticed.

"I'd have thought that marriage was one option."

"Are you recommending it as a cure-all, Mr. Hammond?" she asked, surprised. Then remembered. "I'm sorry. I shouldn't have said that."

"No, no. Fair comment." Brian found himself laughing, much to his own surprise.

She refused a nightcap. Refused a lift home. The house felt very empty when she had left.

Jennifer's evening had been long and empty. Barbara had been out when she had arrived home. She had cooked a meal which she had eaten without tasting. Watched a television programme without seeing it. Read a magazine without taking anything in. She was glad when Barbara came home and they could sit together with a hot drink.

Barbara was bubbling over. She had been to a good concert. Elton John. It had been great. She fingered the pendant at her throat. That was great, too. It was great of Mrs. Hammond to give it to her.

Jennifer disliked it on sight. She knew immediately whose gift it was.

"Do you like my present, mum? I think these are real stones. It's probably worth a bomb."

Jennifer's voice was flat. She knew she was spoiling Barbara's pleasure in the gift but she couldn't help herself. "She's trying to take you away from me as well."

Barbara didn't see it that way. "Mum, she's just trying to be nice, that's all."

"I'm going to bed." It was no good. Barbara didn't understand. Edward didn't understand. Nobody understood. Nobody except Mary Hammond.

CHAPTER EIGHT

Life has a strange habit of paying us back years later for things we have done and almost forgotten about. If you had asked Edward Hammond about Eddie MacDonald, he would have thought a moment then told you that he was a very competent long-haul driver with a quick temper. The quick temper had cost him his job. Eddie MacDonald's version was different. He had worked for Robert Hammond cheerfully and well. But no man could retain his integrity and work for Edward Hammond. It was chance that had led him to apply for a job with Carter Express.

It was not chance which led Harry Carter to invite him into his office on this fine, sunny morning. Harry Carter, like Edward Hammond, believed in doing his homework. He was smart, Harry Carter. A small, wiry Australian who had made money not always by the accepted standards but by his own. He dealt fairly with his men and paid them well. They liked him. He wasn't one of your high-falutin' bosses who might be able to strip assets but couldn't strip a gear-box. He was just like one of them. With more money, of course.

Harry placed a bottle of malt whisky on the desk. That was the drink for a Scot. Eddie downed his in one. Harry re-filled the glass. He was not drinking himself.

"Now what's this Dave Hammond like?" Harry abbreviated everyone's name immediately. David would wince later when he met Carter and became Dave.

"He's not so bad at his job. So I'm told."

"And Brian?"

MacDonald shrugged. He didn't know. "Can't say. I was only in his office the once. To pick up my cards."

"He's married?"

"Aye. Bit hard. But sexy," MacDonald grinned. "So I'm told. But I hear they've split up now.

That was interesting. "Who left who?"

"I think she left him."

"For another bloke?"

"I wouldn't know." MacDonald sat back. Carter poured another drink.

"And Edward?"

"Not a patch on the old man. I told him that to his face."

"When he fired you?"

"He didn't fire me. I walked out." MacDonald was incensed. Carter could stuff his whisky.

It was the right reaction. Now MacDonald would talk. "Why did you walk out, Eddie?" The question was put sympathetically. Carter was on his side. Carter genuinely wanted to know.

"I told you when I came here. Too many chiefs there now. Not enough Indians."

"Four of them on the Board. Right?"

"Aye, it's a real square dance."

"Tell me something else. . . ."

"I'm a driver. Not an information bureau." MacDonald was feeling a little drunk now, a little aggressive. He had been aggressive the night Edward Hammond had fired him. Carter had no intention of firing him.

"You're not doing any driving today, mate." He pushed the bottle towards MacDonald. "You're having a day off. Right? Now what about the bird – Jennifer, is it?"

"Not your type."

"She was left twenty-five per cent, right? Twenty-five per cent and a seat on the Board. Why?"

MacDonald knew he was being used now. But the whisky was good stuff. He didn't get it very often. "I'm just a driver . . ." It was a mild protest.

"She was the old man's secretary. Right?"

"Well . . . maybe a bit more than that."

"Yeah?"

"It's just gossip. . . ."

"That's right," Carter agreed. He winked suggestively. Both men laughed. MacDonald no longer cared. He had no loyalty to the Hammonds. Why should he?

"You can work that one out for yourself," he said.

"I'm ahead of you. This daughter. Whose is she?"

"Whose do you think?" They both laughed again.

Carter stood up. He'd got what he wanted. He put the cap back on the bottle and pushed it to MacDonald.

"Beaut, Eddie. Take that home with you."

He grinned as MacDonald lurched towards the door. An hour to go to lunch. He was well able to take care of himself at this little bean-feast. He whistled a few bars of "Waltzing Matilda", as he combed his hair. Winners are made not born, he decided.

Jennifer Kingsley was not at the lunch. She was at home feeling distinctly unwell. Edward had telephoned to insist she attend. Barbara had taken the call and told him in no uncertain terms that her mother was not working that day.

"What did Edward say?" Jennifer was taken aback.

"He sent you his love." Barbara grinned at her mother. She seemed very grown-up now. The parent-child relationship had been reversed almost overnight. Now it was Barbara handing out the advice and asking the questions.

"Is it over with you and Edward?" It was the question which Jennifer had been asking herself. She answered the way a daughter would answer a mother.

"Do I pry into your relationships?"

"I haven't got any. But you used to."

"When you were sixteen."

"Well, now, I'm eighteen. Old enough to vote. Officially registered as an adult. Still, if you don't want to talk about it. . . ." She picked up a magazine.

"Then at eighteen you should know that relationships aren't that easy to define."

"But you're not going to marry him any more?"

"Did I ever tell you I was going to?" It was a feeble attempt. Barbara was both too young and too old to accept the deceit.

"Not in so many words. But there were all sorts of heavy hints going around."

"Well I'm not." Jennifer had to say something. It was best that the decision not to marry appeared to come from her. It was a face-saving answer.

"Plenty more fish in the sea."

"Barbara, you're being thoroughly obnoxious. The sooner you go to Art School, the better."

"That's all right. I'm moving out Saturday and I just wanted to know how things stood before I did."

They avoided each other for the rest of the afternoon. Barbara found things to do in her room. Jennifer rested and wondered how the lunch had gone.

Edward came to tell her. He came to her for comfort. Carter had beaten him at his own game. He wanted to tell Jenny about it. And he wanted to see her. He missed her. He liked having her there at business lunches and board meetings. He had come to count on her. Nancy. Well, he had picked up with Nancy where they had left off. Before Jenny. But it was still Jenny. Edward was old enough and experienced enough to know that he could spend the rest of his life enjoying himself with women who were younger, prettier, sexier than Jenny, but in each of those women, he would be looking for her. His first love. His last. He brought arum lilies.

Jennifer burst out laughing when she saw them.

"What's funny?"

"Arum lilies. I'm not dead."

"It was the only thing on the stall that looked fresh." He was hurt.

"Well, thank you. I'll just put these in a vase." She went off to fetch one.

Edward was still standing up when she came back. She started to arrange the flowers.

"Sit down and tell me how it went."

"Oh, er, do you want to talk business?"

"You want to. And I want to. I'm feeling much better."

They both sat down and Edward told her about the lunch. Carter had arrived with a man he introduced as his financial adviser. Michael Harris had sat in silence throughout most of the discussion. Edward had plunged straight in with the offer: that Carter Express be administered by Hammond Transport under the one roof and the land adjacent to the depot would be bought at a reasonable price by the combined company.

"Take-over." Carter did not like the idea.

"Merger," Brian put in.

Carter said they were the same thing. David had explained the difference.

"You'd still be operating your short-haul delivery service as a semi-autonomous unit."

"That's a lovely word, Dave. Now tell me what it means." Dave had winced at the diminutive and Edward had laughed.

He and Carter had the same approach. He told Brian to explain the deal to him.

"We would assume financial responsibility for all your trading costs, including present liabilities – outstanding customer debts, outstanding payments on plant and capital equipment, pay off outstanding bank loans and overdrafts."

Carter had amazed them. He was not in the least worried that they knew his troubles. He told them he could take care of his problems himself. He explained that he might have five overdrawn bank accounts but he also had a thick order book. He was not worried that he had no capital. He was still bidding for the land because he had a private loan. Edward had jumped in then.

"From a bunch of sharks who'll have the clothes off your back the moment you default?" he had asked.

It was then Harris spoke for the first time. "My company is happy to make the loan, Mr. Hammond. And I should warn you to beware of slander."

Carter had turned down the offer flat. They had all had a large brandy and left.

Edward laughed. "I like him. Carter."

Jennifer did not like the sound of him at all. "You said he was a villain."

"But he admits it."

"And that's the sort of man you wanted in the firm?"

"We all have to sail close to the wind sometimes, Jenny. He just sails closer than most."

Jennifer got up to pour a drink. "You *have* changed, haven't you?" she asked.

"I'm learning." Edward did not see what she was getting at. "Never too old for that."

"Learning what?"

"How to be honest in a devious way."

"You mean smart."

"Borret's taught me a few lessons in that."

Jennifer looked at him. Could one be totally wrong about a person? Could a person be totally fooled by another? Was it really impossible for people to say what they meant, be honest with each other? She asked him. "In some ways the Hammond reputation for straight dealing was always a bit of a sham, wasn't it?"

"Over money?" Edward was surprised.

"Over people."

It took a moment or two for Edward to work out what she was getting at. When he did, he didn't say anything.

"How's Nancy?"

"Jenny, come on. . . ." Edward did not want to talk about Nancy. He wanted to talk to Jenny.

Jenny smiled sadly. "Back to the sham."

Edward was annoyed. He had played fair with Jenny after all. "You wouldn't even have known who she was if I hadn't told you."

Jenny's voice was even, controlled. "You mean if your mother hadn't told me."

"What?" Edward could not believe his ears. "She doesn't even know about Nancy."

"Why, were you ashamed of her?"

"It just wasn't any of mother's business."

Jenny shrugged. "She's certainly made it her business now."

Edward's thoughts were beginning to connect. How could his mother have told Jenny about Nancy? She knew nothing about Nancy. But Jenny wouldn't make up a story like that. He had to establish he'd heard correctly.

"My mother told you about Nancy Lincoln?" he asked slowly and clearly.

"Yes. On the phone."

Edward slammed down his glass. The prospect of a pleasant evening had been destroyed. His mother's work. "Thank you," he said and left.

He did not go straight home. He didn't want to go home. He wanted time to think. Time to bring his anger under control so he could deal with this situation. Time to drink.

He drank quite a lot but his anger prevented his getting drunk. There was to be no sentimentality tonight. His mother's actions had been unforgivable. He had not married Jenny immediately as he had wanted because of the threat of his mother's having a heart attack. Tonight, she could drop dead at his feet and he wouldn't care. He hated her in that moment with the deep hatred you can only feel for someone you love deeply.

Mary Hammond was totally unprepared for the confrontation. She had talked to Brian that day. Ann had visited her at her request. She felt now that Brian would be happier with Ann after all. And she would not lose her grandchildren. Ann had seen through her little game. Ann always did. Nevertheless, the possibilities seemed hopeful.

She was drinking a soothing cup of hot chocolate when Edward arrived. She offered to make him one. His reaction was almost rude. She supposed he had been drinking. Business troubles perhaps.

"Ann came to see me today," she said mildly.

"At whose suggestion?"

"Well, mine really. As you probably know, she and Brian were undecided about whether to send the children to boarding school."

"And where do you come into the picture, Mother?" The tone was ironic, insulting even.

"I offered to help."

"I'll bet you did."

"Is there any reason why I shouldn't?"

"Does Brian know you've seen Ann?"

"Not at the moment...."

"That seems to me to be a very good reason."

"Have you been drinking, Edward?"

"I've lost a slip of paper. A slip of paper with a telephone number on it. Nancy Lincoln was the name. Remember, Mother? Remember how you phoned that number? And how you then rang Jennifer to tell her? Remember?" His voice was raised now. Mary did not like the reference to Jennifer. Edward knew he must not mention that woman in this house. He was forgetting himself.

"What of it?" she asked.

"It was none of your business."

"If you think that I'm sorry. But there's not much I can do about it." Mary looked tired. She felt a little alarmed. But she did not feel afraid. She knew her eldest son. Or thought she did.

"But there is something I can do, Mother. I'm packing my things tonight and I'm leaving this house tomorrow morning. You can then sit here, night after night, in this big empty house and scheme away to your heart's content. But no one is going to give a damn!"

He turned his back on her. Mary swallowed back her tears. She tried to retrieve the situation.

"I hope you will apologise in the morning."

There was no answer. She couldn't get through to Edward in this mood.

"Edward," she said, "Where will you go. . . ." There was no answer. She had to know the worst. "Edward . . . not, not to that Kingsley woman."

Edward still did not say anything.

She staggered slightly as she left the room but he still did not move. She was crying silently. What would she do now? She had lost her husband. She had lost her grandchildren. And now, it seemed, she had lost Edward. She seemed to be a born loser.

Brian's evening had been most pleasant. He was sitting with Pamela Graham in a modest restaurant having a splendid time. The modest restaurant had been her suggestion. She was an odd girl. He'd seen her quite by chance. He had been driving past the school and she was leaving late having stayed on to mark some papers. At least he told himself it was chance. It was, however, the first time he had taken that particular route home. He had offered her a lift home. He had stopped outside his house and suggested a sherry. She had accepted quite calmly. They had chatted pleasantly enough and he had found himself explaining that he could not talk to Ann. She had listened sympathetically. She was a good listener. A good talker, too. She talked only when she had something interesting to say. That was quite often. When he had suggested dinner at the Trellis, she had said it was too expensive. They had settled for Mario's and he had promised not to discuss his marital problems. The suggestion was his, not hers.

By the time they had decided on their order, he hadn't wanted to talk about his marriage anyway. He not only didn't want to think about Ann, he had forgotten her. He was happy.

It was funny, he thought, leaning back and looking at Pamela's face – animated, they were talking about music – his mother seemed to have changed her tune during their conversation that afternoon. Last time he had seen her, she had surprised him by saying that form without substance was no basis for a marriage. Today she had said that she was alarmed by disorder and broken marriages seemed to her a symptom of a disordered world. He had answered that perhaps the word was not disordered but fluid, with old marriages re-forming into new ones.

She had questioned him about that. Wondered whether he was thinking of marrying again. He had replied it was just theoretical. Now, he wondered. Had he been thinking about Pamela Graham? He recalled what his mother had said.

"I suspect new marriages bear the indelible print of the old ones. . . . We don't change ourselves with our partners."

We don't change ourselves. . . . That was true enough. But had he ever actually been himself with Ann? He had abandoned his interest in music. Not done so many things he would have liked because she had not shared his enthusiasms. Ann had been herself in their relationship. She had done, said and bought what she had wanted. It was he who had made the compromises. He was always the loser. With another person, he would not change himself – he would change into what he really was. With the right person, that is. He smiled at Pamela.

"Would you like to go to a concert with me some time?"

Harry Carter was still leaving nothing to chance. He had turned down the Hammond offer flat. He was playing for terms. With a nudge in the right direction from Michael Harris. He grimaced. He knew what he had to do and he knew with whom. David Hammond was his man. Tonight Dave was coming to a party at his place. He had had to be lured, of course. The bait was Sally Woolf.

The Hammond brothers were expecting an approach. David was rather flattered that it was he whom Carter had singled out to put the offer to. At first they had been surprised that Carter had brought Harris along to lunch. Then they had worked it out. Harris had insisted on coming along. He wanted to hear the terms of the offer. The Hammonds were safe collateral for another loan. If Carter also had an outstanding debt with Harris's firm, they might force him to accept.

The hypothesis was correct. Carter owed a lot of money. He needed more to pay off his debts. He had deliberately made an offer for the spare land knowing the Hammonds would have to approach him and talk business.

David left for the party with strict instructions to listen to the new terms and then let Carter sweat overnight wondering whether they would be considered.

Sally Woolf. Now, how on earth did Carter know Sally, David mused. Sally was Sir John Borret's personal assistant – very personal and very helpful. She had used David, used him to get information, used him sexually. David bore her no grudges. He had thrown over Jill because of Sally. The choice was between a fluffy kitten and a man-eating tiger. He had received a few scratches and maulings along the way but that sort of woman attracted him. He liked living dangerously.

Harry Carter had the sort of penthouse flat that only someone on the verge of bankruptcy could afford. David was impressed. The decoration was ultra-modern, the books bought by the yard and two exceptionally sexy-looking girls had obviously been delivered with the furniture straight out of the advertisement. They were introduced as Olga and Dee-Dee, not the names their parents had bestowed on them some eighteen or nineteen years previously and, like all girls of their type, they appeared to have no surnames. They acknowledged the introduction with small, cooing noises and went on listening to the music.

Despite himself, David was impressed. His business might be in trouble but Harry certainly led the good life.

"What can I get you?" Carter asked.

David tried to think of something which Carter wouldn't have.

"Don't suppose you'd have schnapps, would you?"

"No problem." Carter rummaged behind the bar. David might have known.

"What's happened to Sally?"

"Going to be late. You know Sally."

"How did you come to meet her?"

Carter poured the drink. "Same way as you, I imagine. Through Borret's. They tried to pull the same stunt on me as they did to you. Two years back."

"Do you have much contact with Borret's, now?"

Carter's answer was deliberately casual. "John and I play the odd round of golf, you know, but there's no hard feelings. John's a good loser."

He had made his point. John, not Sir John. And he had obviously won his little encounter with Borret's. David grinned.

They were like two animals circling round each other. The two girls lit cigarettes then settled back again.

Carter re-filled their glasses. He tried to explain his situation to David. "I've always been a loner, ever since I was a kid. Hated the idea of people telling me what to do. Then one day you wake up and think – what's it all about? I'm a one-man band, so what? What's so bloody marvellous about that?"

"How much do you owe Harris?"

Carter shrugged the question aside. "He's no problem, mate. I've dealt with ratbags like him before."

"But he's on your neck," David insisted. Whatever else he was doing, Carter was certainly not running scared.

"Dave," he said, "let's get this straight. I can go in with anyone anytime I like. Or I can stay as I am."

"Then what's your proposition, Harry?"

Carter smiled. "You're making the propositions, not me."

"We've already made ours – over lunch."

"You missed something out."

"Did we?"

Carter nodded. "A seat on the board."

At that moment the music changed. Strident rock belted out from the speakers. Olga got up and started to gyrate, alone but looking all the time at Carter. Without a word, he got up and led the way through the french windows and on to the balcony. David hesitated for a moment watching the sinuous movements, then followed. They leaned out on the parapet and looked at London.

"What's happened to Sally?" David wasn't letting Harry off the hook.

"Doesn't look as though she'll make it."

"You surprise me," said David, unsurprised.

"Do I get that seat or not?"

"Why do you feel you need it?"

"It's normal. Anyway," he said cockily, "you need me."

"We do?" Now David was surprised.

"Four directors on a Board? You get two for two against. Deadlock."

"Ted has a casting vote."

"Right. So all he has to do at any meeting is to pick up one vote – say, Jennifer Kingsley?" David did not react. "And you and Brian are outvoted every time."

David chose his words carefully. "And you think that's the way it happens."

"Dave," Carter put a hand on David's shoulder. "You know my set-up and believe me, I know yours. All of it."

The two men looked at each other hard. They both had a lot to think about before one of them knew he had won.

CHAPTER NINE

Mary Hammond and Jennifer Kingsley were experiencing similar emotions. They were facing up to losing someone. Barbara was leaving home. Edward was leaving home.

Jennifer hated the thought of Barbara's leaving. The house would be empty without her. If she were honest with herself, she would admit, too, that she was worried for Barbara. She had left home at eighteen and look what her life had been. She had never regretted her love affair with Robert Hammond. She was proud of it. She cherished its memory. Loved the daughter of that liaison. But that wasn't what she wanted for Barbara. She wanted Barbara to have fun, to meet a nice boy, to marry him. It is strange that we never want our own children to have the lives that we have. If we honestly think they can do better, why should we accept second best for ourselves? She pushed the thoughts aside.

Barbara had been up since six packing her things. She was acting deliberately casual. Her mother had looked unhappy lately but she refused to feel guilty. She had to live her own life. She was sharing a flat with two other girls. She was looking forward to it and yet at the same time, she was nervous. It was a big step.

"I can't think why you're moving from here to go and live in a flat that's just as far from Art School as we are. What's the point?"

"I'm leaving, Mum. Tomorrow morning. There's nothing else to talk about."

"Do you have to be unpleasant about it?" Jennifer snapped. "Have I made your life such a misery for the last eighteen years?"

Barbara was glad her mother was unpleasant. It would make the leaving a little easier. Her mother was sorry she had been unpleasant. It made the leaving more difficult. Barbara sensed it.

"Don't worry, Mum. I won't be far away. Anyway, I'll see you later today. I'd better buy some outrageous clothes now

I'm an art student," she grimaced. "I'll call in to the office later, shall I?"

It was an olive branch.

"All right, Barbara. But not till later. There's another board meeting this morning."

"Another? When do you do any work?"

They laughed together.

"Well, I'd better go." Jennifer got up.

Barbara watched her leave. If only Edward were still around. That would make everything simpler.

Mary had got up early as usual. She had spent an uneasy night. She could not believe that Edward would keep his threat. She decided to act as though the previous night's scene had not happened. Things looked normal enough. Edward was standing in the middle of the living-room scanning the headlines as he did every morning. Then he would fold the paper and take it with him to read in detail over his coffee. As she came into the room, he folded the paper.

"Have you had breakfast, Edward?"

"No. I'll get some in the canteen. I'm off now."

"Will you be home for dinner?"

Edward looked at her. He had never denied his mother anything. Until now. He did not flinch at what he had to say. "Most of my stuff is packed. I'll do the rest this evening if that's all right with you."

"But, Edward, don't just go like that. . . ."

"Mother," he was impatient to be off. "We talked this out last night

"No. You talked. . . ."

"And I was rude to you. I apologise for that but nothing else changes."

Edward turned and walked out of the door. Out of her life. Mary sat down. It wasn't possible. It wasn't happening. It was a bad dream and she would wake up. What did it matter that she had telephoned Nancy Lincoln? It was a mother's natural concern. Just because you got older and your children got older and led their own lives didn't mean that you weren't still their mother, always there to help.

She wasn't sure how she got through the rest of the day. The realisation that Edward really had gone came when Tom Parker arrived unexpectedly. He refused lunch but accepted a glass of sherry. Tom and Joan Parker were old friends of herself and Robert. Tom was one of Hammond's oldest clients. He had put a lot of business their way over the years.

They exchanged pleasantries, enquired after each other's health, told each other how well they were looking. And then Tom asked whether there would be a chance of a word with Edward if he called back later that evening. This was it. Now she had to face the truth. She did not know when Tom could see Edward because she didn't know when she would see Edward again. She prevaricated.

"You know Edward. Works so hard. I'm never sure. Maybe it would be best if you called him at the office."

"Too damn hard he works. Like his father. Ought to delegate more. Have a bit of fun. Remember those holidays we used to have, Mary. We had some good times then, the four of us."

Mary remembered. Those long, golden days that had gone forever. Tom Parker had always been the life and soul of the party. He made money and he took the time to spend it. Joan had never spent hours waiting for Tom to come home.

"I would have liked to see Edward," Tom was saying. "There's a spot of business which is just in his line and it would be quite a favour to me. Building materials on this new council contract. It's a big job. Still, I'll try to ring him later."

He refused a second drink and left.

Mary's other visitor that day was not only unexpected but unknown to her. Harry Carter had decided the meeting that day would definitely give him a seat on the board. Anticipating success, he was now planning its celebration. He liked the idea of Hammonds. He could do big things with it. It was a family business so he decided to meet the family.

Mrs. Wheeler had shown him into the hall. Harry had walked into the living-room. Mary was surprised to see him there. She thought he was the man who had come to fix the cooker. Amazingly enough, this small, to her unprepossessing man with the appalling accent, introduced himself and said he was joining Hammonds. It seemed as though the world was going round without her.

They chatted about Harry's life and homeland. He lounged back, obviously prepared to go through it month by month and town by town. Mary made polite noises and showed him to the door. There he turned and made a startling proposition.

"Would you like to come to a party at my place tonight, Mrs. Hammond?"

"A party, Mr. Carter?"

"Just for the Hammonds. A get-together, you know."

"A party for the Hammonds?"

"Yes, that's right."

"It's a long time since anyone invited me to a party." Mary's first instinct was to refuse. Then she thought again. A party for the Hammonds. She was a Hammond. She would go. She smiled and accepted.

Ann Hammond arrived while Brian was eating breakfast. He was reading a newspaper and listening to the news so for a moment he didn't realise she had come in. She wished him good morning and helped herself to coffee.

"It's very early."

"Yes, I was in town overnight."

"Oh, where did you sleep?"

"I beg your pardon?" Ann looked at him in feigned surprise. Brian shrugged. He supposed it was no longer his business.

The telephone rang. Ann leapt to take it.

"Yes, darling. Good morning. Yes." Brian wondered who the hell she was speaking to. She handed him the receiver. It was Carol. He talked a few moments with his daughter then put down the phone.

"You told the children you'd be here?"

"Yes."

"All night?"

"Of course. What did you expect me to tell them?" Ann was unrepentant.

"And that's the only reason you came here this morning." Brian was disgusted. "As an alibi for the children."

"No. I came to sort this school business out once and for all."

"But I thought you'd already made up your mind about that."

Ann pouted. "All right, if you're quite happy about it."

Brian as usual was disconcerted by Ann's lightning changes

of mind. He looked at her helplessly. "Look, there's a board meeting, Ann. Can I see you later? Dinner?"

She smiled. "Fine. The Trellis?"

He smiled back. She did look marvellous. "Seven o'clock. I'll get Marion to book the table."

Stale from their domestic crises, Edward, Jennifer and Brian sat round the board-room table. Despite a fair intake of alcohol the night before, David was fresh and eager to get down to business. He explained Carter's terms.

"A seat on the Board and voting shares . . ."

"That's what he's after, is it," said Edward drily.

"Which is more or less what we were going to offer him anyway."

"Salary?" asked Brian.

"Didn't mention it. I suspect he's got a suggestion up his sleeve."

"Such as?" Edward asked.

"I don't know. He may be after a lump sum and a percentage on turnover."

"Then he can forget it." Edward snapped.

"I'm just guessing.

Jennifer was trying to catch up. Yesterday, Edward had told her that Carter had rejected their offer. Now David was talking as though it were imperative Carter be seduced into joining Hammonds.

"Has he been offered a seat on the Board?" she enquired.

"He's been offered nothing so far," Edward replied.

"But you intend to give him one?" she pressed.

"That's reasonable," said Brian reasonably.

"And voting shares – where do they come from? Are you suggesting we each relinquish some?"

"No, no," said Brian. "We're not talking about Hammond Transport shares but shares on the new company, the combined company of which Hammond Transport becomes the major shareholder."

Jennifer still did not understand. "But I thought you said that Carter was keen to join up with us so why do we have to offer him anything?"

"To be fair," said David. "He does have something to offer us."

Jennifer looked at all the brothers in turn. "I just don't understand. Yesterday you were talking about the tough deal you were going to make. Today you're falling over backwards to be fair. What's changed since yesterday?"

"Nothing's changed," David said. "Except that I've now had a chance to talk to him informally . . ."

So that was it? All boys together. Jennifer was annoyed that business tacks should have been changed so fast and at the same time felt that jealousy that women executives feel of men who seem able to share a drink and seal an alliance in a way that women never can.

"You mean over drinks at his place?" she said hotly. "And after a couple of drinks you've decided he's really a good bloke after all and all the tough talk of yesterday evaporates. Typical of men and their so-called tough bargaining ability. It's all a pose."

Edward brought the meeting to order. "Right. Let's get this sorted out calmly. Jenny?"

She apologised. "I'm sorry. I just want people to be consistent."

"Brian?"

"Carter will want some compensation. I'm merely trying to suggest something that doesn't cost us money."

"David?"

"I'd go further than that. He knows his own side of the business better than we do. I think we need him on the board."

"Do you agree with that?" Jennifer asked Edward.

"No. As it happens, I agree with you. Let's try and get him for nothing. David, ring Marion and ask her to show Mr. Carter in."

Harry Carter bounded into the room, beamed all round and placed a pile of folders on the board-room table. Without waiting for an introduction, he went straight over to Jennifer and shook her hand.

"Great pleasure to meet you at last, Miss Kingsley."

Jennifer deliberately let her hand go limp.

"Sit down, Carter." Edward was being at his most chairmanlike.

Carter beamed at them all again. "I can't stop. Bad day. You know how it is."

David was furious. "Last night you told me you had a proposal."

"That's right. One copy each." He passed round the folders. "Obviously you're going to need time to study it. So when you've done that, give me a call. Perhaps after lunch?"

"You could have sent them round by messenger," Edward was furious. He was being beaten at his own game again.

"No trouble," said Carter innocently. "And it was a pleasure to meet you, Miss Kingsley. Heard a lot about you." He looked at Jennifer hard. She felt a sudden stab of apprehension. He beamed round at them all once more and left.

Carter's proposals were brief, succinct and beautifully presented.

"Typical. All flashy cover and nothing inside," Edward grumbled.

David was impressed. He recognised the value of a good promotion job. "So here's the crunch. Directorship, twenty per cent of the shares and. . . . good God, he'll be lucky. Some salary he's asking for."

"Drop him," said Edward. "Let him come back on his knees."

"I agree," said Jennifer.

"We'll meet again after lunch to discuss it formally," Edward dismissed the meeting.

Barbara was waiting in her mother's office, full of excitement about her new safari jacket. She was showing it to Harry Carter. Jennifer could scarcely believe her eyes. What on earth was he doing here with Barbara? He grinned at her cheekily. He knew what she was thinking.

"Met this beautiful young lady and knew she must be a chip off the old block."

"Do you think I look like mum?" Like most young girls, the thought of resembling her mother, pretty though she was, did not appeal to Barbara.

"No. You're the spitting image of your dad."

Jennifer froze. Barbara warmed to Carter immediately. She still wondered what exactly her father had been like.

"Did you know him, Mr. Carter?"

"Bob Hammond and I were great mates."

"I don't remember seeing you here before, Mr. Carter," Jenny said coldly.

"Not here, no. Transport caff down at Eltham. Used to play snooker with him."

"Did he tell you about me?" Barbara asked eagerly.

"Always on about you."

Jennifer interrupted. "We'd better have a quick lunch, Barbara. I've a lot to do."

"But I want to hear about this . . ."

"Mr. Carter is exaggerating. It seems to be his stock in trade."

"But he knew . . ."

"I met Bob Hammond plenty of times, Miss Kingsley."

Jennifer deliberately started to put on her coat. Carter smiled at Barbara.

"I'm having a party at my place tonight. I'm inviting all the Hammonds. We may have something to celebrate. If not, we can always commiserate. I hope you'll both come?"

Jennifer tried to find an excuse. She didn't want to go. She didn't want to be with this man at all. But Barbara was too quick for her. Barbara wanted to see him again, find out what she could from him.

"I'd love to," she said.

"Beaut," said Carter. "Seven o'clock then. And see if you can persuade your mum to let her hair down."

Jennifer put off lunch with Barbara by the simple expedient of giving her some money with which to buy the trousers that went with the jacket she'd bought. As soon as she had left, she marched into Edward's office. She was upset and angry. Carter had deliberately checked her out and then dropped the information in front of Barbara.

Edward was surprisingly unmoved. "These things always get out. People love to gossip. You must know that."

"I don't expect complete strangers to walk in here . . ."

"He's been checking out on us. So what?"

"Into our private lives as well."

"We checked on his."

"It's disgusting, whoever does it."

"No. It's embarrassing maybe. But the information's no use to him."

"Who knows what he can use? Or where else he's been sniffing around?"

She was close to tears. Edward put his arm round her. "Don't get yourself upset, Jenny. I thought you'd learned to live with this."

Jennifer shook her head slowly. "No, not really. I'm sick of being baited." She turned away and went back to her own office.

When the board meeting re-convened, each had read Carter's proposals and decided what they were going to do.

Jennifer was pro Carter. Jennifer had changed her mind completely. She had been upset by Carter but more upset by Edward's reaction. If he didn't care what business methods they used or were used against them, then Hammonds was not Hammonds any more. She was wrong. David was right. They needed Carter.

Brian was pro Carter. For financial reasons. He knew that if Hammonds didn't take Carter, Borret's would. Borret's had a contract with Hammonds. When that ran out, they would need vans. Carter had vans. But, more important, if Carter bought the land adjoining the Hammond depot and they bought Carter . . . He would vote for it.

David was pro Carter. His dream was expansion, new business. Carter seemed to talk the same language. Edward had patronised David in the early days. Occasionally still, he treated him as a tyro. David's thoughts thrust ahead. They could get bigger, better. There was a whole new world waiting there outside.

Edward was biding his time. He had had to accept his brothers and Jennifer into the family business. He would not easily accept the business taking in an outsider. He had a vote and he had a casting vote. With Jennifer's vote, he did not have to take Carter. David and Brian had argued fluently – they would vote for Carter. It was obvious.

Jenny had sat back and listened quietly. Now she came into the discussion. Edward was amazed. She seemed to be on Carter's side.

"You've completely swung round from this morning. Why?"

"I told you earlier. I think we need him."

"But I thought that was temper."

"I think he'd act as a useful catalyst. That's all."

"I don't even know what that means." When faced with a

situation he didn't like, Edward often resorted to the pretension of ignorance.

"Yes, you do." Jennifer looked at him coolly.

"So do I. Let's put it to the vote." David was jubilant. He didn't know why Jenny had come round and he didn't care.

"Wait a minute . . ." Edward looked at them all. "I'm not agreeing that salary."

They took the vote, subject to salary negotiation. The motion was carried.

Edward's face was grim as he reached for the telephone. He dialled Carter's number. Carter was waiting.

"Carter? Edward Hammond. Now listen: my Board has instructed me to accept your proposals in that you are offered a seat on the Board of Directors and a twenty per cent holding in the new company . . . No, no, wait a minute. It doesn't accept your salary demand or anything approaching it. . . . That's up to you. What we're offering is half of what you're asking, subject to annual review like the rest. . . . I see." Edward smiled grimly. "Well, that's just about the fastest climb-down I've ever known. Well we're all realists, aren't we. In the end." He put down the receiver.

David smiled at Jennifer. "Are you going to Carter's party tonight?"

"No, no, I don't think so."

"Me neither," Brian got up. It was late. He mustn't keep Ann waiting.

Edward looked tired, defeated. He glanced at the three of them then, without a word, left.

Ann was sitting in the cocktail bar when Brian arrived. She looked ravishing. He guessed she had spent the afternoon at the hairdresser. What he didn't know was that Ann had made a discovery that morning. A discovery she did not like. She was bored in the country where her mother was forever trying to lead the conversation round to reconciliation with Brian and the children were under her feet all day long. She had walked out on Brian becouse she was bored. She was still bored. She could live with that. As long as Brian was bored too. What she could not stand was the thought of his being happy with someone else.

The arrival of Brian's first drink and her second precipitated the attack.

"Mrs. Scott does still come in, does she?"

Brian blinked. "Yes."

"Then she's getting very slack. The bathroom was a mess."

"It's only for an hour a day."

"She should be able to get through it in that time."

Brian was not interested in domestic trivia. "I'm quite happy with the arrangement anyway. Let's talk about schools."

Ann ploughed on. "And she can't have done the kitchen floor for at least a week. I've left her a note about that."

"Then you shouldn't have done," Brian said hotly.

"I've also washed up the two sherry glasses for you."

So that was it. Brian understood now.

"There was lipstick on one of them. I don't think that's quite the thing to leave around for Mrs. Scott to find. Do you?"

Brian did not know what to say. He was grateful when the waiter came and he could order a fresh round of drinks and collect his thoughts.

Ann had gone far enough for the moment. She changed tack. "I've got a suggestion. Let Nigel go to boarding school. He wants to anyway. And we'll both discuss it with Carol."

"Haven't you done that?"

Ann sipped her drink. "Of course. But let's do it together now. If you can spare the time. I'm sure you're having a whale of a time. No family to bother with."

"I don't really see why I should have to explain . . ."

"Then don't," Ann said lazily. But of course Brian did.

"Miss Graham came in last night to see Carol."

So that was it. Ann knew about women. She knew the Pamela Graham type. Mousy, dowdy, boring but devoted. Very devoted. And therefore dangerous.

"I would have thought you could do better than that."

"She happens to be a very intelligent woman," Brian sprang to Pamela's defence. That wasn't good.

"It's intelligence that turns you on, is it?" Ann mocked him. "You should have told me that years ago."

"If we're going to quarrel, perhaps we should forget the whole idea."

"There's no quarrel." Ann picked up the menu. "You have

your friends. I have mine. The only difference is, I don't feel guilty about it. You do. Good luck with her anyway."

Brian was suddenly angry. "You really are a bitch, aren't you?"

Ann just laughed. "You're going to miss that."

David was meeting Jill. He was picking her up at the photographer's studio where she was modelling sports clothes. He was looking forward to seeing her again. She had looked marvellous the other night. He had missed her. There'd been a few girls but none of them had had the dangerous qualities of a Sally Woolf or the sweetness of Jill. It was amazing how sweet she was. She was so pretty. She could pick and choose her men. But she had seemed eager to see him again when he'd made the date on the phone. She appeared to bear no grudge that he'd dropped her so abruptly two years ago. He'd buy her a quick drink and then on to Carter's place. She would make Olga and Dee-Dee look cheap and flashy.

Edward sat in his office. Morose. Drinking scotch. He had hoped Jenny might go to the party at Carter's. But she had made it clear she wasn't going to. What had happened to her? She was so damned prudish and boring lately. She never tried to see the funny side of anything. God, a man needed a woman to relax with at the end of the day. He reached for the phone. He would call Nancy and take her to the party. There'd be no problem with Jenny out of the way.

At home in her bedroom, Jenny was getting ready for Carter's party. She didn't want to go. She didn't want to go anywhere. But Barbara wanted to go. It was Barbara's last night at home. She didn't want to lose Barbara. Tonight they would do what she wanted. She sprayed on some perfume.

"Come on, Barbara," she called. "Let's get it over with."

CHAPTER TEN

Harry Carter looked round his flat. He was satisfied with what he saw. It looked expensive, impressive. The hi-fi was giving out sweet music. The champagne was on ice. He poured himself a beer. He had drunk half of it when the doorbell rang. His first guests.

Jennifer and Barbara stood in the doorway. He invited them in and took their coats. They stood for a moment looking round, taking in the scene. No wonder he had made the salary demand he had, Jennifer thought. This flat must cost a bomb.

"Are we the first to arrive?" Barbara asked.

"You won the race, you get the prize. Look at it that way. Champagne all right?" He made his way over to the bar. He took his beer glass and hid it. He took a bottle of champagne from the fridge. It was a very good year for champagne.

"It's my good luck," he said as he poured their drinks. "My first arrivals. I get to have two lovely ladies to myself. Is she really your mother?" he asked Barbara. "It's incredible. You look more like sisters."

This last remark dissolved the slight tension which still obtained between Jennifer and Barbara. They grinned at each other, hardly able to believe that Carter could trot out this corny old compliment in all seriousness.

"I don't believe it," Jennifer whispered to Barbara and in that moment they were like sisters.

"What do you think of this place?" Carter asked, handing them their drinks. "Not bad, is it?"

Barbara thought it was marvellous. "I'd love a flat like this," she said, thinking of the cramped quarters she would be sharing with two other girls from tomorrow on.

"Ah, this is nothing to the unit I had in Sydney," Carter said. He wasn't boasting. He had a healthy respect for the material things of life and didn't mind saying so. "You should have seen it. The top floor of a high-rise and the windows looked right out over Sydney harbour. The view was out of this world."

"Why didn't you stay there?" Barbara thought it sounded marvellous.

"I had some bad luck. The landlord thought I should pay the rent."

They all laughed. Then there was a silence. Barbara made a comment on the music. Carter knew very little about it. He had bought a pile of albums in a shop one day. They were background, nothing more. He poured another drink. They were all relieved when the doorbell rang.

Jennifer's relief turned to dismay when Carter brought in his guest. It was Mary Hammond. That put the damper on the evening altogether.

Mary, as usual, showed superb control. She was beautifully dressed in a long, crepe dress, wearing the pearls which had been a tenth wedding anniversary present from her late husband.

"Good evening, Miss Kingsley, Barbara." She smiled at Barbara.

"Hullo," Barbara smiled back.

Jennifer smiled briefly.

Carter felt ill at ease. Like most Australians, he was more at home with men than women and three women together was a daunting prospect. He had been interested to see what would happen when Jennifer and Mary met. Now he wasn't so sure that it was a good idea after all.

"I don't know where the others have got to," he remarked brightly, rushing to the champagne bottle.

"Perhaps Miss Kingsley knows," said Mary.

"I'm afraid not. I didn't know quite who Mr. Carter had invited."

"I was in the same position, Miss Kingsley."

There, they'd both made their position quite clear. Neither would have come if they had known the other would be there. However, both were here and there was nothing for it but to drink their champagne and make the best of it.

Carter was feeling quite nervous. He was babbling on about his view and saying it wasn't a patch on the view he had enjoyed in Sydney. Mary was listening politely, so politely it was obvious she was bored.

"Mind you, this is only a place to bed down," he said to Mary. "Nothing like your house. Now that's what I call a real home. Got a style about it. You know what I mean."

Mary smiled in acknowledgement. "Well I like it, Mr. Carter."

"I'll bet you made it what it is, Mrs. Hammond. It's got you written all over it." The remark sounded embarrassingly insincere but the truth was that Harry Carter meant it. He respected tradition and taste.

"Of course I knew your husband, Mrs. Hammond," Carter went on.

"Really?" Mary was astonished.

"Oh yes. Bob and me were great mates," he said ungrammatically.

"I didn't think anyone ever called him Bob. Did you, Miss Kingsley? Know anyone, that is?"

Briefly, the two women were on the same side. "No, he didn't like it."

"No, he didn't, did he," Mary said sharply.

"Well, I suppose I'm just an ignorant Aussie. I never asked him whether he liked it or not." Whether this was true or not, Mary and Jennifer could not help finding his candour appealing. And it was obviously heavy going for him surrounded by three women.

"Let's have some more champagne," he said, leaping up and fetching another bottle. "Is it O.K. for you, Mrs. Hammond?"

"Very nice."

"Good. I really go for champagne, you know, drink it all the time."

Especially when you're feeling nervous, Mary thought. Out loud she said, "Really. I was always under the impression that Australians preferred beer."

"Ah, you don't want to believe all that stuff about beer-swilling Aussies. We're not all like that." As though to prove his point, Carter gulped down half a glass as though it were beer and not champagne.

There was another silence while they all dutifully sipped their drinks. Carter couldn't stand it. He put down his glass and got up.

"I'm going to ring them. See what's happened." He strode over to the phone. They all sat and watched as he dialled first one number, then another. There was no answer. He drew his own conclusions.

"They must be on their way. I'd better open another bottle so it'll be ready for them."

While he busied himself at the bar, Mary enquired after Jennifer's health. Jennifer replied she was keeping well.

"I'm glad to hear it. I thought you looked rather strained."

"I expect I've been working hard, Mrs. Hammond. I'm not a lady of leisure. I've always had to earn my own living."

They smiled at each other falsely. Carter groaned to himself as he re-joined them. He had to break this up. Leaving Barbara to talk to Mary about hard edge abstract painting – at least that's what he thought she called it – he drew Jennifer to one side.

"What's the idea? Is it a fix?"

"Is what a fix?"

"Not even a phone call. I'd call that a deliberate slap in the face, wouldn't you?" Carter always went straight to the point.

"It's no use asking me, Mr. Carter."

Carter was irritated. These limeys with their formal airs and casual ways of treating people infuriated him. "Will you, for crying out loud, stop calling me Mr. Carter. I keep wanting to look round to see where Mr. Carter is. Listen, straight up, is it a fix or not?"

"Who do you imagine is being fixed?"

"Me. By you."

"Personally?"

"There are parts of the deal I don't buy. Nothing's signed yet. We could have sorted it out tonight in a friendly fashion. Only maybe they saw me coming and put you up to stall it."

"Why me?"

"You're a woman."

"What about it?"

"I don't fight with women."

Jennifer laughed. She couldn't believe that anyone could be so old-fashioned. Even Edward, the most reactionary of the Hammond brothers, would not hesitate to go into battle with a woman.

"It went against you." Carter continued. "You were outvoted, weren't you. You didn't want the merger. Didn't want me on the Board?"

"Oddly enough, I was on your side."

Harry clinked his glass against hers. "Maybe we're going to get on after all. Let's have lunch tomorrow and see if we can't agree a figure for my salary."

"There's no point. You agree our terms or forget the whole thing. We've made our final offer."

"You do a good hatchet job, Jenny, I'll say that for you. O.K. I'll think about it. Maybe it's worth taking a cut for the sake of working with you."

Mary Hammond was ready to go. She was furious with her sons. She was astonished they should behave so badly even towards someone so ill-bred as Harry Carter. It put them on his level. Harry made a few token appeals to her to stay for another drink but she left. Jennifer and Barbara got up, too. He leaned against the door for a minute after they had all left. God, what a boring evening. Women! He walked over to the fridge and got out a can of beer.

David had had every intention of going to Carter's party. He had picked up Jill on time. She was looking beautiful. One drink had led to another. Then she had protested she was hungry. He wondered how she kept so slim and ate so much. Still he was hungry himself and he couldn't see Carter laying on any food. They called for a menu.

Jill had changed a lot. She seemed more sure of herself. She no longer sat and hung on his every word. She chattered away, telling him about her day and her job. He didn't want to go to the party. He wanted to take her back to his flat.

"Let's have coffee at my place."

"What about this party you mentioned?"

"That? Oh, no sweat. Big brother Edward's going. He can hold the fort." He had to get her back to his flat right now. She looked infinitely desirable.

She smiled and followed him. When they reached his flat, she went straight to the cupboard.

"What are you doing?"

"Looking for the coffee. It's still in the same place, isn't it?"

"Yes. Nothing's changed." He came up behind her and nibbled her ear. Nothing had changed. They could begin where they had left off and they had left off exactly where he wanted to begin. Jill breathed deeply. David still had the same effect on her. He could arouse her with the merest touch. She wanted him desperately. But not this way. She was never again going to be dependent on him the way she had once been.

"I'll make the coffee," she said and moved out of reach.

"All right," David smiled. He put on a record. Blues. So she was playing hard to get? Good. He would enjoy it all the more. The telephone rang but he ignored it. He didn't want any interruption. When it finally stopped, he took it off the hook.

They drank their coffee with brandy. Then they had another. David put his arm round Jill and she rested her head on his shoulder. Her hair smelled nice.

"Come on. We'd better adjourn," he whispered.

"I don't think you should drive," said Jill, deliberately misunderstanding him.

"What?"

"You've been drinking. Will you phone for a taxi, please?"

"Won't your friend be there? What's her name?" David still did not understand.

"Julie? Yes, she'll be there."

"Then what are we doing going back to your place?"

"My bed is there. I've got to be up early in the morning."

David tried again. "I've a very loud alarm clock."

"I'd rather be at home."

"Why this maidenly reserve all of a sudden?" David was annoyed.

It was a remark which stung Jill. "I have a job to do, David. A demanding job, whatever you may think."

"So have I. But I don't let it interfere with my private life."

"When you were giving me the brush-off last year, I seem to remember you telling me the opposite."

"Keeping scores, are we. Playing games?"

"No. I'd just like to go home."

"Fine." David picked up the telephone and dialled the taxi rank. He was furious.

Jill looked at him a little worried. He made no attempt to kiss her good night. On her way home, she wondered whether she had done the right thing.

David lay in bed thinking about her. He had enjoyed the evening. Except for the ending, of course. Still, that was all part of the game. He would phone her tomorrow and suggest lunch. He was still thinking about her when he fell asleep.

Edward meant to go to Carter's party. He had telephoned Nancy with the intention of taking her. At the same time, he felt a little apprehensive at the prospect. He never talked to his brothers about his private life. They knew about him and Jennifer but it had never been discussed openly. He wondered how David would react to Nancy. He was pleased when Nancy demurred at the idea. After all, there was no need for him to go. David would be there.

"Do you think I'll fit in at the party?" Nancy asked, echoing his own misgivings.

"Don't be silly. The thing is, I don't know whether I'd be playing into Carter's hands by going. Anyway, it's nice here." He looked round Nancy's flat appreciatively.

"Is she going to be there? This other person of yours?"

"I don't know," Edward said slowly

"What were you going to prove, taking me? That you don't need her? That you can find someone else just like that?"

That made three of them. Jennifer. His mother. And now Nancy. Edward groaned. "Nancy, don't start analysing me. I'm not in the mood."

"At least phone Mr. Carter and tell him you won't be going."

Edward thought for a moment. "No, there's no need. I can't be bothered making excuses. Anyway, David will be there."

It was one of the pleasantest evenings Edward had spent with Nancy. For the first time they really talked to each other. It was amazing, he thought, how long you could know someone, how intimate you could be with them and yet you didn't know them at all. Whoever said you didn't really know a woman unless you'd been to bed with her was wrong. Totally wrong. That's easy compared with sharing your thoughts.

"Why did you leave your husband?"

"Eventually I realised he was living through me. What I did. What I said. I was alone with him or without him so I thought I might as well be without him."

"And when we met – where did I fit in?"

Nancy thought. "You came along at the right time. You cared about your work and I admired that. You weren't demanding. You didn't care what I did as long as I was around now and then."

"I suppose I used you."

"Yes," said Nancy. "Just as I used you."

"There was a need as well, Nancy."

"That was mutual, too. As you might have gathered."

"What about now, Nancy? Do you have any needs?"

"No. I walked out on a marriage. I was serious about that for a very long time. I'm not ready for anyone serious. Perhaps I never will be. But certainly not yet."

She put things so clearly. He tried to explain his situation to her. "It's all being getting so confused, Nancy. And there was no need. I see that now. I've been behaving like an adolescent. It was stupid. Tonight's been a big help. It's helped me get things in perspective. And I've enjoyed it."

"I've enjoyed it, too."

Edward glanced at his watch. "We've talked, really talked. And now I'm going because I want to think about the things you've said. It's a compliment, Nancy. Do you understand?"

She understood. Edward got into his car and drove home. Home to his mother's house. He had behaved stupidly. Like a schoolboy. He had got angry with his mother about nothing. Just because Jenny chose to issue ultimatums didn't mean he had to break with his mother. And what harm had been done anyway?

His mother was reading when he arrived. They said guarded hellos. Mary's spirits soared when she saw him. The house had seemed so empty when she came back from that dreadful party.

Edward passed off his presence as casually as he could. "Haven't found any place yet so I thought there was no rush. As long as it doesn't inconvenience you?"

It didn't. There was no rush. Edward noticed his mother was all dressed up.

"Have you been somewhere then?"

"To Harry Carter's."

"He invited you as well?" Edward laughed. "He's got a nerve."

"I think he was rather put out when you didn't arrive."

"Something cropped up. I couldn't make it. Well, I'll be off to bed."

She had won. Mary pressed her advantage. "You must introduce me to Mrs. Lincoln one day."

Edward looked at her. She smiled back innocently.

"Why?" he asked.

"I'd like to meet her. A pity she couldn't have come with you to Mr. Carter's tonight."

She'd never give up. So he would. He was tired suddenly.

"Yes. Good night, Mother."

"Good night, Edward."

CHAPTER ELEVEN

The flat was not living up to expectations. Barbara quite liked her two flat-mates but they were both very untidy. Barbara found herself in the unlikely situation of picking up things after them. And it was a long bus-ride from Chelsea. In many ways she would be better off living at home. She would get her laundry done and her meals cooked. And save money.

But art school was all she had hoped it would be. Better, in fact. She had been nervous on the first day. Her new jacket had looked horribly new when she put it on. But what else could she wear? She pulled on her new shoes. They looked horribly new, too. No make-up. Just some lip gloss and dark shadow round her eyes. She'd spend a few days finding out what everyone was wearing. It was still very early but she was eager to get out of the cramped flat.

There were very few trend-setters in the Kings Road at this time in the morning. A middle-aged lady in a middle-aged mink coat was walking a middle-aged poodle. Barbara smiled at her. Surprised, the lady smiled back and went her way thinking that some of these hippies were quite pleasant really although the poor girl had looked very tired; such shadows under her eyes.

There weren't very many people in the school building either. Those who were there seemed to know exactly what they were doing and where they were going. Barbara dawdled around till she found the registrar's office. She was directed to Studio C. She was the first to arrive.

So this was it. She looked round the room. A few drawings were pinned to the wall but otherwise it was quite bare. It was a new year and the studio waited for a new batch of students to put its imprint on it. Barbara opened her case and started to take out brushes and pencils. She wondered what the protocol was. She would like to have the place by the window.

She was totally unprepared for Nicholas Fox. From the way he opened the door and strolled in, it was obvious that he was someone. In fact, it was amazing the door had not swept open automatically before him. Barbara gazed at him.

He was in his thirties. Seen from the back or in a certain light, you might take him for ten years younger. He was slim, tall, blonde. His clothes were casual but beautifully cut. His hair was casual but beautifully cut. He epitomised cool. He couldn't be a student. And yet he couldn't possibly be a lecturer. Could he?

He smiled at her. His teeth were perfect. "Hullo."

"Hullo," Barbara stammered.

"You're early. Who are you? One of my lot?"

So he was a lecturer. And she was one of his lot!

"I'm Barbara Kingsley," she said. Oh, for a name like Zoe van Oosten or Pandora Lascelles. Barbara Kingsley sounded so suburban.

"I'm Nicholas Fox," he said.

Nicholas Fox was going to teach her. Barbara felt like a small boy, an Arsenal supporter, who's just been told that Charlie George is going to show him how to play football. Nicholas Fox!

"I saw your last exhibition," she blurted out. "In fact, I saw it six times. I thought it was terrific."

"Thank you," Nicholas checked down a register of names. "It didn't go too badly. I sold three which is about par for the course. Now, let me see – Kingsley. Oh, that's right, I remember your portfolio."

"Did you see it?" Barbara asked eagerly. "When I came along for the selection interview?"

"I was on the board."

Nicholas Fox had been on the board. And she didn't remember seeing him! Of course she'd been very young then. It was ages ago. Six months.

"I'm sorry. I was so nervous. I don't think I dared look at anyone," she explained, head bowed, not daring to look at him.

"Yes, I remember now why I chose you. What I liked about your work."

"You chose me?" Barbara was taken aback.

"Oh yes. Visiting tutors like me select their own students, Barbara."

Barbara. He had called her Barbara. It was on the tip of her tongue to ask him what it was he had liked about her work when two other students walked in and the private conversation was over.

She discovered what it was a few days later. A few days in which she had thought constantly about Nicholas Fox. She hardly noticed the other boys in the school. Boys, that's what they were. Nicholas was something else. A man, mature, sophisticated. She was standing at the bus-stop dreaming about him when suddenly he materialised beside her. He was driving a very low-slung sports car.

"You're working late?"

"I got interested."

"It's early days for keenness like that. Which way are you going?"

"The station. I'm off to see my mother."

"Hop in." He made no effort to get out of the car but opened the door from inside.

"Thanks." She slid in as gracefully as she could.

"You had a very good art teacher at your school, didn't you?" he asked.

"She was marvellous. How did you know?"

"I can tell by your work. But you'll find it's very different now. You want to develop yourself. Less of her and more of you. That abstract you submitted with your portfolio – what did you call it?"

"Funeral."

"That was you." He glanced sideways at her. "Had you just been to a funeral?"

"Yes."

"I thought so. Who was it? A relative?"

"My father."

He drove on without comment. Barbara suddenly wanted to appear daring and with it. She wanted him to see her as a sophisticate, cool like himself.

"I'm illegitimate," she said as casually as she could.

"In that case you're lucky to know who your father was." A faint smile hovered round Nicholas's lips. Barbara was glad when they reached the station.

Brian Hammond was being deliberately casual. There was no reason on earth why he shouldn't take the road past Carol's old school. Pamela Graham's school. And since he felt like a cigarette, there was no reason why he shouldn't park outside and relax a few minutes with the newspaper. He took in very little of what he was reading. Every few seconds he checked the driving mirror. This was ridiculous. She was probably supervising school lunch or marking books or something. She wasn't.

She came out of the school gate. A breeze caught her dark hair and she brushed it back impatiently. She looked right and left as though uncertain which way to go. He hooted. She turned, saw the car and walked slowly towards it. He jumped out of the driving-seat and opened the passenger door.

"Can I give you a lift anywhere?"

"I'm not sure. I'm not sure where I'm going. I just felt like getting out of school for an hour. What are you doing here?" She always went straight to the point. He liked that. Ann was a mistress of circumlocution. Nevertheless, he didn't answer directly.

"That's a stroke of luck – for me. I felt like getting away from the office and was just wondering what to do. Perhaps you'd have lunch with me?"

She stood for a moment as though giving the matter careful deliberation.

"All right," she said eventually. "But it will have to be somewhere quick."

They settled for a ploughman's lunch in a pub that was near but not so near that a passing parent or pupil might see them.

"I saw Ann," he began. "You know, my wife. Carol's going to boarding school."

"It's settled then?"

"Well, yes, almost. At least, I think so." Brian didn't want to talk about it. He wished there were no Ann at this moment. No Carol or Nigel. Or boring, domestic decisions to be made.

"What's the problem then?"

"Problem? Oh, there's no problem. That's all actually. Except I wanted to ask you . . . had you noticed there's a Mahler concert at the Wigmore Hall this weekend?"

"No."

"I wondered if you'd like to go."

"You could have telephoned. You didn't need to hang around outside the school."

"You could have refused more easily on the phone."

Pamela sipped her cider. "Brian, I'm not a young girl. I'm

single and that's more or less by choice. I'm not on the lookout for the first separated man who comes along."

"I enjoy your company," Brian protested. "There's no harm in that."

"I think you'd enjoy almost anyone's company just now."

"No, that's not quite true." Brian thought of the invitations he turned down from well-meaning friends. He looked at Pamela. "Besides, I think you may be rather lonely yourself, right now."

The remark was perceptive. It was also unwelcome. Pamela hesitated for a moment before replying.

"You can be very direct."

"I can be wrong, too." Brian softened the blow.

She smiled at him. She liked him. She liked Mahler. She wasn't doing anything on Saturday, so why not?

"I'd better be going," she said, standing up. When he dropped her off at the school gate, she accepted his invitation.

Brian drove back to the depot feeling very good inside. The afternoon went by fast. Business seemed to be looking up. Carter had been nominated to the Board, having accepted their offer, and the new land was in the bag. Edward had turned up with news of a big contract. He had seen Tom Parker. Parker wanted as many vehicles as they could spare. It was a big job. It would mean a lot of money. They would have to wait for a while before Parker paid but so what? Parker was their biggest single client. He was an old friend of the family. Any other client would have had an extensive grilling. But not Tom Parker. There was no need to ask him questions. As Edward said. "We can wait a few weeks for payment. It's like having money in the bank."

Brian was sorry when the day came to an end. He felt restless. He didn't want to go home to an empty house. He dropped into David's office; a few drinks, maybe dinner, would be pleasant. David had a date. He hesitated outside Edward's office. No, he'd go home and go through some figures.

He mooched around the house. Somehow he couldn't settle down to work. He poured himself a drink and looked through the television guide. There was nothing that appealed to him. He looked through the entertainments pages, the concert announcements. Tonight. He hesitated fractionally then dialled Pamela Graham's number.

"Hullo, Pamela? Brian Hammond. Look, I thought I might have to work late tonight but it's fallen through and it suddenly struck me that we could just get to the Festival Hall. There's a Beethoven concert. I don't have any tickets but we could try. . . . Anyway, suppose I pick you up anyway. If we didn't make it, we could have a drink or dinner . . . you only had bread and cheese for lunch, you know." He waited, saying a silent prayer. It was answered. Pamela Graham would be happy to accompany him. He promised to pick her up in half an hour. He hummed a few bars of the *Emperor* as he went upstairs to change.

He was halfway upstairs when the doorbell rang. It was damned annoying. He came down again and opened the door. Ann stood there. She was wearing a black leather dress and extremely becoming black fur hat. Brian was aghast. What on earth was she doing here now?

She walked past him, brushing him slightly. He followed in the wake of a heavy perfume. He could almost hear the minutes ticking by.

"Aren't you going to give me a drink?" she asked.

She drank very slowly. Brian kept stealing surreptitous glances at his watch, working out time schedules in his head. Another five minutes, then he could go. Ann drained her glass. He got up eagerly.

"Yes, I'll have another, darling."

Groaning inwardly, Brian poured a fresh drink. Another man would have coped with the situation. Another man would have told Ann that he was going out. But Brian did not know how to handle women. There had been two women in his life – his mother and his wife. He had been conditioned to believing that one's allegiance was to the women who are legally in one's life. He could not ask Ann directly to leave. It was she who had the right to be here in their home. He tried to find out deviously what her plans were.

"You're coming up to town a lot, these days," he said.

"I'm getting a bit bored with the country to tell the truth."

"You should have let me know you were coming," Brian hesitated. That sounded suspicious. "I'd have tidied up a bit."

"I didn't know I was coming. The car's playing up."

"I'd better go and have a look at it."

"Brian, you don't know any more about cars than I do. The garage can deal with it. In the morning."

Brian grabbed his chance. "Yes, all right, the morning. I'll take it in for you and let you know. I'll drive you to the station. You'll just catch the train." He looked at his watch openly now.

Ann was amused. "What sense is there in going home and then coming all the way back? Anyway, I hate trains. I'll stay the night."

"Where?" Brian's question came out as a squeak.

"Curled up on the back seat of the car is one possibility but I'd prefer a bed here. If you don't mind."

Brian didn't mind. He couldn't mind. He didn't have the strength of character to mind.

"No, of course not."

The telephone rang. He jumped up to answer it. He shot a glance at Ann. Now was the chance. After he'd taken this call, he could put down the receiver and say, "Sorry, I have to go out. But you stay here and make yourself comfortable".

It was Pamela. She had telephoned a friend at the box-office and reserved two seats. She was ready, waiting for him. He couldn't do it. He could not go out with another woman leaving his wife at home. He muttered apologies, made excuses. She understood. Of course.

He came back and sat down. He explained the phone call to Ann. "Someone got some concert tickets for me but I shan't be able to use them."

Ann was sympathetic. She told him he should have gone and enjoyed himself. It was terribly unfair.

"I suppose you've got work to do as usual. You should try to keep your evenings clear, Brian. Remember when you used to take me to concerts?"

"Yes," he said shortly. "It wasn't very successful though, was it?"

"I tried to like them," Ann protested. "I wanted to, but I couldn't. I think it's better to be honest and not pretend, don't you?" She held out her glass to him again. Her car stood outside. It was in perfect running order. She had arrived with perfect timing. Brian seemed upset. If it weren't for her, he would be at one of his terrible concerts. This woman sounded like competition. It was lucky Brian loved her. She smiled at him.

"I'll cook us some supper. See what there is on television, darling."

Jill had to let down David Hammond that evening. She wasn't pleased about it. She had been delighted when he telephoned to make the date. She had wondered how he would react to her walking out of his flat. After all, they had had an affair. It seemed stupid not to sleep with each other now when they had done it for so long. But it wasn't what she wanted. And it didn't seem to affect David after all. He had telephoned.

Julie, her flat-mate, opened the door to him. She was not a particularly attractive girl. Her hair hung round her shoulders and looked as though a shampoo wouldn't do it any serious harm. She wore no make-up. Her clothes were very butch – denim trousers and a loose shirt but the figure below gave no doubt as to her sex. A lot of men shied away from her. She came on in an aggressive way. David disliked her on sight.

"Come in, David Hammond." She opened the door. It wasn't until he was inside that she broke the news. "Jill's had to go to the country. She didn't want to but it's a big advertising job and they're shooting at crack of dawn tomorrow. Would you like a drink?"

Without waiting for an answer, she went straight to the drinks trolley. She didn't ask what he wanted either. She poured two large whiskies and plonked them down in front of him. She then brought the bottle over.

Damn! David was furious. He had been looking forward to seeing Jill. He glared at Julie. She raised her glass to him.

"Cheers."

"Thanks." He essayed a smile. "So you're Julie. I've heard a lot about you. You're a photographer, aren't you?"

"That's right. I've heard about you, too, but I wouldn't dream of telling you what. It might embarrass you." She took a healthy swig at her drink.

"Am I in the company of a practised drinker?"

"Have you got anything better to do?"

"No." He drank.

Julie stared at him with the frank appraisal of a photographer looking for the flaws and good points. David was annoyed. He looked straight back at her.

"You're not at all what I expected."

She filled their glasses again. "You're exactly what I expected."

Her manner irritated him. How dare she form an advance picture of him and then say it was right. "Is that bad?" he asked.

"It's not good."

"Would you care to enlarge on that?" he said stiffly.

She would. And she did. "You're a typical husband-to-be pretending to be a play-it-cool man about town."

"You couldn't be more wrong."

"Do you want to leave?" she was challenging him now.

"Not until I've finished my drink."

"I'm never wrong," she said.

"Not about anything?"

"Nothing. Ever."

David picked up the bottle and filled both their glasses. "Well, we'll see."

She matched him drink for drink. But she seemed to stay sober whereas he felt distinctly light-headed. He stared at her. She was a bitch. He'd like to tame her, show her just how wrong she was. He imagined her pinned down underneath him, clawing at him, biting him. He would deal with her. Whatever she did or said, he would show her no pity. She didn't deserve any. She deserved to be taught a lesson. If it weren't for Jill. Jill. He got up.

"I'm going."

"You can't drive in that state."

"Make me some coffee. I'll feel better then."

"I don't make coffee. I'm going to bed. You can sleep on the couch."

"I don't sleep on couches."

"It's very comfortable."

"It's not me."

"Anything else would spoil a beautiful friendship."

"We haven't got one," he reminded himself, not her.

"That's true." She eased herself out of her chair, sensuously like a cat. "Well, the bathroom's over there. And my room's over there." She looked down at him, provocatively.

He put all thoughts of Jill out of his mind.

CHAPTER TWELVE

The men at the Hammond depot greeted the news of the take-over of Carter Express with even more suspicion than the Board. It was Riley who was deputed to see Edward and find out the score.

Edward gave him a fair picture of the situation. Carter's fleet of vans would be housed at the back of the warehouse where new sheds and bays would be built. Carter's drivers would come with him. Edward explained it made good sense to combine the long haul with a van feeder service. Riley didn't like vans. He said it was like handling a swarm of bees. He left to report back to the men.

The first intimations of trouble came a few days later. Edward looked out of his office window. The men were gathered in a knot by the gates. Edward roared for Riley out of the window. Riley turned, made a sign of acknowledgement. He didn't hurry to Edward's office but took his own good time.

"All right. What's going on?" Edward roared.

"A meeting," said Riley unhelpfully.

"Union business?"

"Not official."

"Unofficial meetings on my time," Edward thumped his desk. "Not on your life."

Riley was unmoved by Edward's blustering. He was well used to it. Anyway, as he pointed out, it was the men's lunch-hour.

The point of the meeting was Carter, or, to be exact, Carter's men. Carter employed non-union drivers. The fact that none of Carter's vans had arrived yet was immaterial. The men wanted the situation clarified before they did. They were afraid. Now was the time to air their grievances and fears. There would be another meeting this evening with the rest of the men. By the next day, they would know more.

The first thing Edward saw the following day as he turned into the depot was a sight he did not like at all. A twin line of drivers stood there. Just stood there. Not doing anything, not going anywhere. The men stared at him as he drove past. They didn't move. Didn't say anything. They had done their talking.

Edward parked his car, got out and looked round. Riley was standing apart from the other drivers. Edward recognised the man he was with. It was Reg Turner, a Union organiser. He was a committed man, fair, shrewd, balanced. Edward was glad it was he. He walked over and invited Turner to coffee. Riley followed them as they walked up the staircase. Edward looked at him pointedly.

"What's your problem?" he asked.

Riley was unruffled. "The lads have elected me spokesman."

"Shop steward now, are you?" Edward ordered coffee for himself and tea for Turner and Riley.

He suggested that work should be resumed before their discussion got under way. Riley demurred. They wanted assurances first. Edward went into a long tirade about what people wanted and what they would get. Turner sat through it all unmoved. He was immune to this kind of remarks. When Edward paused for breath, he came in.

"Bill here came to see me last night after the meeting."

"You have been busy, haven't you?" Edward said sarcastically. "So what now? Is it official? Am I dealing with the union?"

"No, no," Turner said. "The men didn't consult the union in this case. I'm here to help if I can. That's all."

"All right then. Who's doing the talking?" Edward wanted this whole business settled and the men back at work.

Riley was infuriatingly calm. "We passed a resolution last night. Whatever's said today, we want Mr. Carter in on it. It's his drivers we're concerned about."

"Look, forget about that," Edward jumped in. "If I bring Carter in, I've got to have the other directors there too. I know what you're talking about. They don't." Had he gone too far? He'd better make the situation clear. "That's off the record," he added hastily.

"We passed a resolution, Mr. Hammond. I'm not empowered to alter it."

Edward was furious. There were contracts to fulfil, lorries to be got on the road. This would put them back a fair bit. Every moment was losing them money.

Turner turned to Riley. "What happens if Mr. Carter isn't here?" he asked. "Will you organise picket lines?"

Riley was non-committal. "Could be."

"It's blackmail," ranted Edward. "That's what it is. Pure blackmail. And the Union can't do a damn thing about it, can it?"

"Mr. Hammond, I've never known any dispute resolved until the two sides got together and discussed their differences."

Edward knew Turner was right. He rang Marion and told her to get Carter and the other three directors to a board meeting in half an hour's time.

Half an hour later, the meeting was in progress. Turner and Riley sat on one side of the table facing the directors. Edward made the introductions. Turner assessed each director in turn. You could learn a lot about a person and how to handle him just by looking at him.

Carter was not pleased to have been dragged to the office so early. He had had a late night on the club circuit and the telephone call had got him out of bed.

"What's this garbage about my drivers?" he demanded.

Turner looked at him closely. Edward caught the look and knew that Carter had created an immediate unfavourable impression.

"Let's hear from the other side of the table first, shall we?" he reprimanded Carter. Carter could not have cared less. He leaned back and glared into space.

Turner outlined the situation. Hammonds had always been a Union company. Although not a closed shop, it had one hundred per cent Union membership. Now Carter Express was being taken over which would operate from the same premises. Carter Express employed non-Union drivers. The men did not like the situation.

"Well, hard luck, mate," said Carter. "I pay good money. I employ good drivers and that's all I want to know. They can join the Brownies for all I care but that doesn't mean I'm going to let the Girl Guides tell me what to do."

This was a bad start, Edward knew. All this tough, virile talk was alienating Turner and Riley. He looked at Jennifer and David. Good Lord, they were staring at Carter in admiration. They couldn't possibly be impressed by such loud-mouth talk, surely?

"Let's lay it on the line right from the start," Carter went on.

Turner interrupted him. Turning to Edward, he asked if this

was an expression of Company policy, in which case there would be no point in continuing the discussion.

"It was a personal opinion," Edward reassured him.

But Carter was not to be denied. "I'm entitled to say what I think. These fellows might just as well know where I stand right from the off."

Edward could have choked Carter. Turner half-smiled. He didn't mind these rantings too much. He had heard enough of them in ten years of working for the Union. Anyway, from his point of view, a divided opposition was no bad thing. Edward shook his head in disbelief. Turner winked at him. "Perhaps I could suggest a tea-break, Mr. Hammond," he said.

The ten minutes' break gave everyone a chance to relax, to talk generalities. It was a good move. They resumed, slightly more kindly disposed towards each other.

Jennifer did not see the point of the dispute. "Carter's men are van drivers, not lorry drivers," she pointed out.

"There's nothing to say some of them won't get Heavy Goods licences," said Riley.

"Some of them have already," Carter announced.

"There you are then," Riley triumphed.

Jennifer still did not see. "But they'd be treated exactly the same."

Turner explained. "Right, Miss Kingsley, in which case they'd be taking advantage of benefits which the union has secured over the years without accepting any of the obligations."

Carter was contemptuous. "Union benefits. Can't these fellows stand on their own two feet?"

Edward had listened carefully, making occasional notes. Now was the moment for him to negotiate. He addressed himself to Turner. "Listen. You're interested in the welfare of the men, right? Well, we've just been given a big contract by Tom Parker. We want every vehicle we can put on the road. There'll be all the overtime any man could want. If we've got some damn silly unofficial strike going on, we'll lose that contract and the men won't get their overtime."

It was the first Carter had heard of a big contract. "Who's Tom Parker?" he asked. Jennifer explained he was their biggest customer.

David had been thinking hard. He saw himself as a mediator, a man who could talk to the men. He had what he thought was a brilliant thought. "Look, this is all a non-argument, a complete waste of time. Under the Industrial Relations Act, a worker can belong to a union or not. It's entirely up to him. An employer can't force anyone to join a union. So there's nothing we can do about it anyway."

He sat back, feeling rather pleased with himself. Edward groaned inwardly. He was well aware that David had not yet grasped the realities of industrial life.

"There's a hell of a lot they can do about it," he said, indicating Turner and Riley.

Turner took up the gauntlet. "No one's pressing for a closed shop. As you've pointed out, that would be against the law."

"That's what it sounded like to me," Carter broke in.

Turner dismissed the interruption. "Then you haven't been listening, Mr. Carter. No, what we've got here is a situation where men are concerned about the prospect of working alongside non-union drivers. That concern might express itself in unofficial action."

It was time for Brian to speak. "You're the ones who raised all this," he said to Turner and Riley. "What's your solution? Have you got one?"

"Maybe," Turner was deliberately non-committal.

"What?"

"A good old standby. The status quo."

Everyone was puzzled. Everyone except Edward. He now began to see where Turner was heading.

"What does that mean in plain English?" Carter sounded very Australian.

"In plain English, Mr. Carter, there were no difficulties between men and management before the proposed merger between Hammond Transport and Carter Express. So if the merger did not take place, the cause of friction would be removed." He paused to give his words a chance to sink in. "Mind you, now that we're aware of Mr. Carter's views, we might seek a meeting with Carter Express and see if we couldn't persuade him of the error of his ways. But as far as Hammond Transport was concerned?" He turned to Riley.

Riley spoke for the Hammond drivers. "We'd have no quarrel with that. It's only his drivers we're bothered about."

Turner was playing it shrewdly. He turned to Edward next.

"There would also be difficulty about the starting date for your contract with this Tom Parker." Edward felt sick. He cared about the Parker contract. It was one of the biggest jobs Hammonds had been offered.

Carter felt furious. Nobody told him what to do. "If you think I'm going to sit here and listen to threats like that, mate, you've got another think coming."

Edward intervened. He knew what he had to do. He proposed an adjournment. He wanted to talk to Turner and Riley alone. He left the board room with them.

Carter knew what was going on. "Big brother's cooking up a private deal on the side."

"Doing what?" Jennifer couldn't believe it.

"Do we count or don't we?" Carter looked round at them all. "Because if so, maybe we'd better do some private talking too."

Edward went straight to the point. He asked Turner for a proposal. Turner prevaricated, said he thought that was what they had done.

"Don't give me that status quo rubbish. You don't dictate our business. Not yet, you don't."

Turner was mild. "I was simply drawing attention to some of the difficulties which might arise. I thought you took my point, Mr. Hammond."

"I took your point all right. And so did they. Only I know what you're up to and they don't. Come on. What's the deal?"

Turner was reasonable. "Suppose you kick off?"

"I don't see how we're going to solve this today," Edward said. "It'll take time but I want the men back at work. I've been making some notes." He handed a piece of paper to Turner. "I've put down proposals. They're alternatives so don't try and screw me for all of them. Whatever we decide, I've got to sell it to my people, just remember that."

"His people" were waiting for him in rebellious mood.

"What took so long?" Carter asked.

"Trying to talk sense."

"We've been talking too," said Jennifer.

"Well?"

He might have known. They'd got themselves all worked up.

They weren't going to be dictated to. Who runs this business – us or the men? It was blackmail. It was a matter of principle.

"When it comes to business, mate, I'm the boss," said Carter. "I don't want any self-appointed bunch of drivers pushing me around."

"If we give in to them, we've admitted that they have the upper hand." Jenny had been brainwashed all right.

"They'll think they can demand what they like in future and get it," was David's contribution.

Edward swore. "You don't understand, do you? We can't operate without drivers and the drivers don't like something we're doing. Just try and grasp that simple fact will you, stop talking as though you were defending the barricades. Because, by God, you will be if you go on like that."

"They're bluffing. They'll back down," Carter retorted.

"Go and look out of the window. Go on. Look. Use your eyes. Suppose we do what you want. Who's going to be bluffing? Us? Or them?"

Carter was looking out of the window. "They're waiting to be told what to do. If we stand firm, they'll cave in."

"You mean you feel like a fight," Edward said tersely. "Well, I don't. I've outlined some proposals I think they'll accept."

The others looked at each other. They were in no mood for compromises or proposals. They had talked with each other while Edward had been making his private negotiations. They didn't want to know.

"I'm against," said Carter.

"I think if we explain the situation to the men again, they'll see reason," Jennifer put in.

David was unhappy about the whole thing. "We might just be postponing trouble."

"We'd gain time." Time was what Edward wanted right now. Time to get the Parker job under way.

"It might be best to face up to it now," David was unconvinced.

Edward tried the emotional appeal. It wasn't like him. It wouldn't convince Carter. It might persuade his brothers. And Jenny. He asked them to trust him. Carter didn't like the situation. He totted up which way the vote would go on

Edward's proposals. It might be a split. In which case, Edward as chairman had the casting vote.

"Don't try swinging that chairman's casting vote stuff," he warned.

"I'm not going to because you're not on our Board yet," Edward reminded him.

"Hammond Transport are in favour of these proposals by a majority vote. Carter Express are against."

Carter got the picture now. "Hang on, mate. Just a minute . . ."

Edward swept on. "You can either go along with us or if your principles get in the way, you can withdraw from the proposed take-over. That's the position."

Carter stared stonily at Edward. "The blackmail habit seems to be catching. Is that your idea of democracy? Riding roughshod over anyone who doesn't agree with you?"

"You've got a free choice. Make up your mind."

"Let's look at your proposals first." Carter picked up Edward's notes.

It was some time before Turner and Riley were sent for. It had been a stormy session. Edward had had to compromise. But he had won. Just. He put the Board's proposals.

"We've considered very carefully what you had to say and this is our reply. We reject out of hand any suggestion that the men or the union have any right to interfere in any proposed acquisition by Hammond Transport of Carter Express. Further, it is our opinion that the fears expressed by the men are groundless. However, we wish to place on record our belief in the orderly conduct of labour relations. To that end, we make the following offer . . ."

Turner was busily taking down the details. Edward began again after a short pause to clear his throat.

"One. An assurance that we are in favour of union membership for all heavy goods drivers. Two. A further assurance that as from today, Mr. Carter will co-operate with any recruitment efforts and there will be no discrimination against union membership." He looked up at Turner and spoke informally in contrast to the formal negotiating language he had been employing. "In other words, it's up to you, Reg. Progress in this area to be reviewed after a reasonable period."

"What's a reasonable period?" Turner put in.

"Don't try and pin us down. Let's see how it goes, that's all we're saying. In return for these assurances, we shall expect an immediate resumption of work at the Hammond Transport Depot."

Turner and Riley conferred together quietly. They caught the phrase "reasonable expression of goodwill". Edward was nervous. Had they been reasonable enough? Finally, Turner looked up.

"Mr. Riley will put your proposals to the men, Mr. Hammond."

"I can't say how they'll take it, mind." Riley was his usual cautious self.

"What more do they expect?" said Carter. "Do they want us to stand on our heads?"

"Apparently." Edward was shocked. Jennifer still seemed to be siding with Carter.

Lunch dragged on interminably. Nobody spoke. They were all wondering what the decision would be. Each of them went back to their offices and pretended to get on with work.

The two things happened at the same time. Turner and Riley walked into Edward's office and there was the rumble of an engine as the first lorry left the depot. The men had accepted the proposals.

"Well, we've got that little lot sorted out," Edward was jubilant.

"For the time being," Turner warned him.

"One bridge at a time." Edward refused to entertain gloom.

"They've agreed to go back to work, Mr. Hammond," said Riley, "but they're not happy about it."

"We've lost nearly a day when there was no need for it. I'm not happy about that either."

Turner made his goodbyes and he and Riley left.

Edward was disturbed by Jennifer's alliance with Carter. He had come to count on her in meetings to show a reasonable point of view. That was, to take his side. He decided to invite her for a drink that evening. It would be good to see her again.

She wasn't alone. Carter was sitting on the edge of her desk. Edward hesitated for a moment then plunged in.

"Fancy a drink later, Jenny?"

"I'm afraid I've promised Harry . . ."

"Come and join us, mate. You're welcome."

"No thanks. It's not important."

"Up to you." Carter stood up and grinned at Edward as though he knew what he was thinking.

Edward telephoned Nancy and took her for a drink instead. He had an uneasy suspicion that he was using her. But she didn't seem to mind.

CHAPTER THIRTEEN

David had been worried ever since the night he had spent with Julie. His blood ran cold at the very thought. Would she tell Jill? Surely not. After all, she had betrayed Jill just as much as he had. She was Jill's flat-mate. She shouldn't have seduced him. And she had seduced him. He could see it all clearly now. The whisky, the taunts – all calculated to arouse him. She had certainly succeeded. He couldn't remember such an exciting night ever. How long had they made love? Three, four hours? And it had been good each time. Christ, she'd better not tell Jill.

Jill sounded happy to hear from him. She wanted to do some shopping in Chelsea on Saturday. He invited her to tea followed by an evening out. She would not have accepted if she knew, would she?

She arrived hidden by a pile of packages. He took them from her and she smiled at him, pleased to see him. It was all right. He could relax. She waved a carrier-bag in his face.

"I've brought tea with me. Just in case."

He liked the look of her in his kitchen. She started to butter scones and put cakes and biscuits on plates. He went up to her and kissed her lightly. She kissed him back. He tried to take her in his arms but she avoided him. He looked at her, worried. No, she was still on her hard to get kick. She obviously didn't know.

"I shall start over-eating out of sheer frustration and it'll be all your fault," he said, taking a chocolate finger.

"Then you'll get fat and no one will love you."

"No one loves me now, darling." David was playing for sympathy.

The kettle whistled and the doorbell rang at the same time. For a moment, David was terrified. Visions of Julie on the doorstep floated before him. He was not pleased to see his mother but at least it was a relief. "Come in, Mother," he said. "Let me take your coat."

Mary had come to see David on an impulse. She was not the sort of person who calls without ringing first. And normally she would never visit David, knowing his penchant for girls and not wishing to know what he did with them. However, she had spent the day behind a stall at a fete for her favourite charity and she was tired. She needed a cup of tea.

Jill came to greet her. David made the introduction unwillingly. The less his mother knew about his girlfriends the better, as far as he was concerned. Mary was impressed by Jill. Such a pretty girl. And so well-spoken. Exactly the sort of girl she would like as a daughter-in-law. It was time David settled down. She accepted tea. David took in the cosy picture of his mother sitting next to Jill and went to telephone a theatre about seats. Mary could be very warm and understanding when she wanted to be. She quickly ascertained that Jill had known David for some time, that they had lost touch but met again by accident. They seemed to be happy together now. It was all very promising.

David returned to hear his mother inviting Jill to tea. He knew he had to break this up.

"Jill's a working girl, Mother. She's a model. She doesn't get much free time, do you, love?"

If either Jill or his mother caught the warning note in his voice, they ignored it. Without knowing it yet, they both wanted the same thing.

"Do you know, I thought your face was familiar," Mary smiled at Jill. "I must have seen your photograph in the magazines."

"Probably."

"Do you keep copies?" Mary asked. "I'd love to see them."

"I've got most of them."

"Perhaps when you come to tea. No, the next time you see David, give him the ones you like best. I'll return them, of course. Now, David you won't forget, will you?"

"No, Mother, I won't forget." David could not say anything else. But he had a feeling that he was caught up in a situation from which he would find it very difficult to escape. His mother had taken it for granted he would be seeing Jill again. If he were to break with Jill, his mother would ask him about it. She was the first girlfriend of his that Mary had met. He wished he had not invited Jill to tea. He ignored the fact that he had invited Jill to his flat in order to avoid seeing Julie at hers.

It had taken Brian a long time to persuade Pamela Graham to see him again. He had telephoned, of course, the very next day to apologise and try to explain. She had insisted that it was perfectly all right. She understood and, no, she didn't think it would be possible to see him again. He tried to cajole her but to no avail. It was several days and a lot of telephone calls before she finally agreed to meet him for a drink.

He had had time to think in those days. He had had an unpleasant scene with Ann. When he had eventually gone to bed on the night of the ill-fated concert, he had found Ann sleeping in what had once been their bed. He had spent the night in Nigel's room. He had wanted to sleep with Ann. That wasn't the point. If it had been an attempt at a reconciliation as Ann had said the following morning, it was not going to take place on that level. It would be properly thought-out, not decided on the basis of a simple sexual need. He had tried to explain this to Ann. She had reacted in her normal way. "You're so logical and reasonable all the time, you always think there's a reason for everything. Sometimes I do things and I couldn't explain why to myself, let alone you."

"Like taking the children and leaving me?" Brian could not understand the sort of spontaneous action which paid no heed to the anguish it might cause another human being.

"I just know that I want to do something or I have to at a particular time. That's all."

"You're an egoist, Ann. Your philosophy of life is to treat self-interest as the foundation of morality."

Ann didn't care. "I don't have a philosophy of life," she shrugged. "I just want to live, to be alive. Not to feel as though I'm half dead all the time."

She had gone again. He had asked her to telephone should she decide to come up again.

She had not liked that. Her voice had been low when she answered but firm. "This is still my house, Brian, just as much as it is yours."

God knew what she wanted. She obviously didn't know herself. But in the meantime, he felt he was threatened. How could he invite Pamela – anyone – to the house if there was a risk Ann would turn up? He had all the disadvantages and none of the advantages of marriage any more.

Pamela had agreed to meet him in a local pub. He arrived in good time and ordered himself a lager. It had been a thirsty day. He thought for a moment then ordered a large medium sherry. He found a corner table and sat down to wait. She arrived five minutes late. It had been a long five minutes.

He stood up to greet her, uncertain whether to shake hands or not. In the event he just stood there and said, "I didn't really think you'd turn up."

She looked at the glass of sherry. "It looks to me as though you were extremely confident about it."

"Oh that," Brian smiled and she thought again what a warm smile he had. "That was a sort of hostage to fortune. A way of touching wood. Apparently it works."

"When you rang and said you'd be here tonight if I cared to come, I didn't intend to meet you. I still don't think it will serve any purpose."

"At least it gives me the chance to apologise properly."

"There's no need."

"I didn't know that Ann was going to arrive."

"She's your wife. She has every right to."

"I'm not sure about that since it was she who left me. That's the way it was."

"I guessed that." It wasn't said insultingly, quite the opposite. "You don't seem to me to be the sort of man who would sling his wife and children out of the house neck and crop."

They smiled at each other and the moment of tension was over. But Brian had misjudged the situation slightly.

"You and I have things in common, Pamela," he said. "There's no reason why we can't be friends. I love talking to you."

"Brian, I teach at a private, fee-paying school. I have to consider what the parents' attitude would be to a teacher who was meeting a married man."

"A separated man. There's a difference."

"Not to most parents. Especially when your daughter was at that same school until not so very long ago."

Brian fiddled with his drink. He didn't really like long drinks. "There's nothing between us that anyone could object to, Pamela. I think we could be good friends. There's nothing wrong with that."

Pamela decided not to pursue the subject any further for the moment. She was trying to convince herself anyway. She liked Brian more than she cared to admit. She had given herself all the arguments she had just given Brian to persuade herself not to see him again. She had also employed Brian's arguments to justify seeing him again to herself.

Brian picked up her glass and went to the bar. He came back with another sherry for her and whisky for himself.

"I can't manage more than one beer," he explained. "After that, I have to go on to shorts."

"Perhaps you've never been really poor."

"No, I suppose not. Often short of money though."

"A struggle to run two cars and find the school fees. My heart doesn't bleed for that sort of middle-class poverty." Pamela seemed to be deliberately needling him.

"That's a bit contradictory, isn't it? Since you choose to teach at a private school?"

"Perhaps I see what you do to your children."

Brian was silent. The remark had hit home. He missed Nigel and Carol. He was genuinely worried about them. Pamela sensed his hurt. She was sorry.

"I'm a contradictory person," she said gently. "I shouldn't have come tonight. But I did. Since I did come, I should have left after one drink. But I haven't."

"Now what? Are you going home?"

She looked at him, surprised. Was he planning to get rid of her so quickly then? Brian realised she had misinterpreted his remark.

"I was hoping you'd have dinner with me."

"I see." She hesitated. "I shouldn't."

"I don't see why not."

"All right," she said.

She had committed herself now. This would be no light flirtation. On the other hand, what else could it be?

Barbara had agonised for days after Nicholas Fox had given her a lift to the station. Had she sounded ridiculously phony with all that stuff about being illegitimate? After all, she could hardly expect someone like Nicholas to be impressed by that sort of thing. Apart from lectures, she had not seen him again. All the girl students in her class were obsessed by him, working particularly hard to please him, but he didn't single any one out for particular attention. So it had been a surprise when he had asked her to stay behind one afternoon.

"You're shaping up nicely," he had said. "How about a drink tomorrow? About seven in the Bell?" He had left without waiting for an answer.

She arrived ten minutes late deliberately. She sometimes went to a pub at lunchtime with the other students but she hated the idea of being alone in a bar. Nicholas was there when she arrived, a gin and tonic in front of him on the bar.

"Hullo," he said, checking his watch. "You're late."

"Only ten minutes in case you weren't here. I didn't want to wait around in a bar on my own."

"Why not?" Nicholas didn't understand. In his world, women did what they wanted. There were no ground rules, no restrictions. Barbara felt very young and unsophisticated.

"What do you drink?"

Barbara remembered the party at Harry Carter's. "I like champagne," she said.

"And I fancy a Lamborghini. What do you drink?"

Barbara settled for a sherry. They drank in silence for a while. They were both thinking the same thing. That is, Barbara wondered why he had invited her and Nicholas wondered why he had invited her. As a visiting lecturer and not a member of the staff, he had often taken out girl students. But he usually went for the girls who were older than their years, girls who had been around. Barbara was a funny girl. She had talent, but, then, so had lots of students. She wasn't the prettiest girl he had taught but she had a quality of vulnerability which appealed to him. Vulnerable yet at the same time she had a directness about her. He pushed the thought away. She was a pretty girl. He fancied her. "Have another drink," he said.

"I've still got some left. . . ."

He ordered another round. He asked her a few mundane questions about her flat.

"Have you got your own room?" he asked suddenly.

"No, I share with another girl."

"That's a conversation-stopper if ever I heard one."

"Why?" Barbara genuinely didn't understand what he was

getting at. He dropped the subject. Time enough for that some other night.

"When's your next exhibition?" she asked.

"Two or three months time."

"Where?"

He groaned. "The trouble with art students is that they always want to talk about art."

"Don't you?" Barbara was amazed.

"Not all the time, no."

Barbara tried to think of some other subject which might interest him. She came up with one that interested her.

"Are you married?"

"Why?"

"I wondered."

"No."

"You're not the sort?" She could see him dedicating his life to art.

"I have been married. Twice."

"Oh." She'd have to change that picture.

"Fortunately, they've both remarried so it doesn't cost me anything." Barbara didn't seem to understand. "I don't have to pay maintenance and all that stuff."

"I see."

She fiddled with her glass. Nicholas looked at her. If only she'd relax. This was really getting very boring.

"Are you afraid of me?"

"No," she tried to laugh. It came out as a nervous laugh so she pretended to cough instead. "I'm nervous, I suppose."

"Why?"

"I don't know. I just am."

"Did you drive here?"

"No. Why?"

"It's time we went and I don't feel like driving you home. I'll find you a taxi. Come on." He put down his glass and turned away. Barbara swallowed the rest of hers and followed him. He glanced back over his shoulder at her. She looked upset. He had to make an excuse. "I've got an elderly aunt staying with me and I ought to go and talk to her."

"I see." Barbara saw very well. He was obviously bored. He wouldn't have invited her just for a drink. He had probably meant to take her out for dinner but couldn't face the idea after half an hour in her company. He would probably never ask her out again. Next time she would think of lots of things in advance to talk about. She would be poised and scintillating. Except there wouldn't be a next time. She'd never see Nicholas Fox alone again.

CHAPTER FOURTEEN

Life for Jennifer Kingsley had become a bleak and barren passing of the days. At work, she and Edward seemed forever to be on opposite sides. At home, the evenings were bleak and barren too. It was funny really. If Edward were still around, she would have been happy for Barbara to be sharing a flat. She would have welcomed the opportunity to be alone with him, eating dinner, watching television. That was part of life she had missed. That home life with a man before the children came along. Barbara had come and gone and now she was completely alone. She resented it. She was too young to spend evening after evening doing nothing. She suddenly realised how few friends she had. A woman who is the mistress of a married man has no time for other relationships. She has to keep herself available for when he is available. She hadn't minded then. The nights alone had been spent thinking about their time together, anticipating the next time. Even washing her hair or ironing had been a pleasure because she was doing it for someone. For him.

When Barbara telephoned to say she was coming back home to live, Jennifer was delighted. Barbara listened for a while and then started to talk terms. She wanted complete freedom. She didn't want to be restricted in any way but to come and go as though she were living in a flat. Jennifer acquiesced. How our children can hurt us, she thought. Barbara talked as though she had been living in a prison for eighteen years. But she was pleased to have her home again. It was good to get up in the morning and cook breakfast for two. To watch television and be able to share opinions about programmes.

When Edward telephoned to ask whether he could come round to see her, she was doubly delighted. Perhaps everything was going right at last?

Their greetings were a little strained. Funny how quickly friends become strangers. Jennifer poured herself a drink and found her hands were shaking. They had none of the small talk others have. They couldn't even ask each other what kind of day they had had. They had had the same kind of day.

Edward was as nervous as she was. He was grateful when Barbara poked her head round the door.

"Hullo, stranger," she said. She didn't mince words.

"What are you doing?"

"I'm off. A date." She grinned, waved and vanished.

"Where's she going?" Edward wanted to know. He suddenly realised that he worried about Barbara as a father might.

"Out with her tutor. Nicholas Fox."

"What's he like?"

"I haven't met him. He's a painter. Barbara thinks he's wonderful. He's a lot older than she is and that's all I know."

Jennifer looked so worried, he wanted to take her in his arms and comfort her. He wanted to talk to Barbara, find out who this fellow was. But he didn't have that right any more. Jenny would rebuff him as she had done so often lately. She was finished with him, she'd made that quite plain. What he had to do now was make sure the business didn't suffer.

"Jenny, I've been thinking," he said. "It seems to me . . . well, we can't go on like this. Snapping at each other all the time."

"I didn't know we were."

"Oh, come on, you know what I mean."

"Because I try to get you to see things clearly?"

"To see things the way you see them, Jenny. That's not the same."

"So you want to tell me I'm wrong. Is that it?"

"No, I don't want to tell you anything. I just think it's time we faced up to what's happened. There was something between us. We enjoyed each other's company. I liked it and I shan't forget it."

"You sound as though you were talking about something dead."

"Not dead. But it is in the past now, isn't it."

If Edward had put it as a question and not as a statement, there might have been a chance, but he didn't. And as it wasn't a question, Jennifer could not answer.

"I don't want to spoil something that was good," Edward went on. "Go on bickering, have it all turn sour. For instance, there's no point in me asking you out when you're busy all the time, or going home early . . ."

"I'm not instantly available, Edward," said Jennifer, stifling the memory of the nights she spent alone in this room.

"You used to enjoy spending time with me."

"I used to be sure of you."

It was Edward's chance to say something. But he didn't either.

"If there's no future in it. After all, we may as well face it."

"Well, if you've decided that."

"It was you who changed things," Edward reminded her.

"I asked you for as much consideration as you give to your family."

"I'm not going to be told what to do."

"You did exactly what you were told to do and you weren't told by me."

"Let's not start again." Edward did not like the thought that he had kow-towed to his mother.

"Edward, just what are you saying?"

"We see each other every day. We've got to go on working together. All right, it didn't work out and I'm sorry about that. But at least let's be friends. That's what I'm saying. I don't want to upset you any more. That's why I thought we'd better sort out where we stand."

It was a long speech for Edward. Jennifer felt he must have rehearsed it. It wasn't what she had wanted to hear. She had been hurt by Edward and she had reacted against that hurt but she had never meant things to end. Not like this. But Edward had obviously got over her. She could only accept what he said. That was what women had to do, wasn't it? It was men who decided when to begin and end relationships.

The evening stretched frighteningly ahead. Jennifer did various tasks about the house, taking as long as possible over them. She felt sure the clock must have stopped at one point but it hadn't. She wondered where Edward was now and what he was doing. And with whom. There was no point in such thinking. She had to forget Edward, wipe him out of her life as he had wiped her out of his. She wondered what Barbara was doing. Nicholas Fox. Even the name perturbed her. It sounded dangerous. She didn't like the thought of Barbara's going out with older men. Was it her fault? Was Barbara looking for a father figure?

The clock chimed midnight and Barbara still wasn't home.

Jennifer didn't know what to do. She couldn't surely be much later than this. After all, it was a week night and bars and restaurants had to close some time. Where could she be? She would be furious if she waited up for her. She had better go to bed.

She read in bed then tried to sleep. It was no use. She switched on the bedside lamp. It was half-past two. Barbara hadn't come home yet. She was sure of that. She put on her dressing-gown and went to investigate. Barbara's room was in darkness. Barbara wasn't there. Jennifer went downstairs. As she reached the bottom, Barbara's key grated in the lock. It was too late to go back up again. Anyway, Jennifer had to talk to her.

Barbara was walking on air. The evening had been the most wonderful evening of her life. She would never forget it. Nicholas Fox had asked her out again. He had told her he enjoyed her company. They had had drinks and a meal, seen a film and then he had invited her back to his place for coffee. He had the most marvellous studio she could ever have imagined. It was perfect. He was perfect.

Jennifer brought her back to earth with a bump. She didn't want to see her mother tonight. She wanted to get straight into bed and dream of Nicholas. Jennifer looked grey and tired and worried.

"Hullo. I thought you'd be asleep."

"Where have you been?" Jennifer was worried sick. She knew she was handling this badly but she couldn't stop herself.

"The cinema. I told you," Barbara turned away.

"Until this hour?"

"Then we had some coffee."

"It must have been an all-night coffee bar."

"It was." Barbara looked at her mother. She had spoiled everything. Now she was going to pay. "But we didn't stay there. He's got a super flat with a studio."

"You didn't say you were going to be out this late."

"I didn't know. We decided as we went along. The time just sort of drifted away."

"You could have phoned."

"Oh, Mum, you'd have been asleep."

"I've been lying in bed worrying. I didn't know what had

happened to you. You could have been taken ill, or involved in an accident or anything."

Barbara realised her mother was genuinely upset, and she was sorry. What she couldn't stomach was the hypocritical arguments she had just heard.

"That's not what you were afraid of, is it?" she asked.

"I don't know this man. I've never even met him. I know you think you're grown up because you're eighteen but you're not."

"Not because I'm eighteen but because I feel grown up now."

Jennifer paused. Was there some special significance in that use of now? Had she imagined it or had Barbara used the word to tell her something?

"I'm only thinking of your own good. I don't want to see you hurt, that's all. You're my daughter. I can't just say nothing when I see you making mistakes."

"What mistakes?"

Jennifer blundered on. "This man's much older than you are. He's probably married."

She had used the wrong arguments for the right reasons. She had played into Barbara's hands.

"He's not married. Not now. Anyway, Robert Hammond was married, too, wasn't he? Or was that different somehow?"

This couldn't be true. Her own daughter was putting her on trial. Jennifer lost her temper.

"It was different, if you want to know. Robert wasn't someone who was on the look-out for a pretty new student he could impress and then drop when it suited him."

"What was it in his case? The pretty new secretary?"

"Don't speak like that. He was your father."

"How was he my father? Was he here when I was growing up? I didn't even know about him until he was dead."

"That was my doing, not his."

"Just don't talk to me about older men, that's all."

Was this what she and Robert had done? Created this child, so like them both in so many ways, who now resented them both. Surely there were words which could explain. She tried again.

"Barbara, we had a very special relationship which lasted nearly twenty years. We did what seemed right. We preserved his family but we loved each other and between us there was respect and affection and consideration. I met him as a girl, grew into a woman and when he died, you were nearly grown up. And all that time he was the only man in my life and I don't regret any of it and never will because I think I was lucky. Lucky to have known that sort of love."

Jennifer's eyes misted over. She honestly believed what she had said. Not to believe it would mean she had lived a lie for twenty years. It takes a special sort of courage to admit one has made a mistake. Barbara, as an outsider, a "stranger", according to the name Robert Hammond had chosen for her, could see another argument. She was young, member of a generation which prided itself on its honesty and spared nobody.

"That sounds fine, Mum. But the fact is you met a married man with three children and you had a long-standing affair with him when he could get away from his wife and family. Well, anything I do is going to be in the open. There'll be no deceit and no secrets. I'll tell you, yes. But you've no right to try and tell me what's right and what's wrong. You're in no position to judge."

There was nothing else to say. The two women stared at each other. They were both emotionally and physically spent. Barbara muttered something about being tired and went upstairs. Jennifer looked for her cigarettes, sat down and lit one. She felt unreal, amorphous. Funny how a woman is defined by her relations to other people: she had been a mistress, a mother, Edward's fiancee. Now Robert was dead, Barbara had rejected her and Edward had walked out on her. She was just a woman and in this moment, she had no strength to accept the challenge to make anything else of herself "Oh Edward," she cried silently. "Why couldn't you have understood?"

If she had only known it, Edward had been asking for her understanding. The things he had wanted to say and the things he had said had been totally different. Different because he had not learned to read a woman. He took things at face value. Jennifer did the same. The result: stalemate.

He took refuge with Nancy Lincoln. Nancy understood. He was lucky to have her. This time, he would play it straight. Make it plain to her what the situation was. To his surprise, she didn't react as he had hoped.

"I've sorted things out, Nancy," he said, raising his glass to her.

"What things?"

"I went to see her. That's why I'm here to tell you about it. We were just letting things drift. It's much better to face up to things, don't you think?"

"That's up to you." Nancy sounded totally unconcerned.

"You see, I felt that if it wasn't going to lead anywhere after all, it was much better to admit it, not to go on pretending that it was going to be all right in the end."

"Edward, why are you telling me this? It's nothing to do with me."

"Of course it is. I did it for your sake as much as anyone's." Edward was pleased with himself. What woman could resist the thought that a man had done something so dramatic for her? Nancy could.

"Then you shouldn't have done," she sounded irritated. "If you had anything to say to her, it should have been because you wanted to say it."

"Well, that's true to some extent."

"All right. But please don't tell me about it because I'm not involved. What you do with your life when we're not together is your affair, not mine."

He wondered what had got into her. He wasn't in love with Nancy, never had been. But he liked her. They got on well together. She talked sense. Edward liked the company of women. If he couldn't have Jennifer, he wasn't going to become a misogynist. Life had to go on, after all. He had planned a day out for them both on Sunday – a trip to the Cotswolds with a good lunch, dinner on the way back. He couldn't believe it when she said she wasn't free. Even more incredible was the reason: she was going to see Simon, her husband.

"Put him off to another day," he suggested.

"I'd rather not. I'm a bit worried about him. He sounded rather depressed and upset."

"You left him a long time ago. He's nothing to do with you now."

"He's a part of my life. I can't rub him out entirely even if I wanted to."

"I'm not asking you to rub him out. Just to put him off to

some more convenient time so we can have a pleasant day out together."

She was adamant. "I'm sorry, Edward, but it's not convenient for me. I've promised Simon now and I prefer not to break my promises."

Edward looked at her. It crossed his mind that this all bore a vague resemblance to another occasion when he wouldn't do what Jennifer wanted. He had lost Jenny as a result. Was this how she felt, the way he was feeling now? Was it impossible to be loyal to anyone without being disloyal to someone else?

CHAPTER FIFTEEN

I'll turn off at the next corner and go home. I'm only driving over here because I want to check out that new restaurant off the High Street. It's a pleasant evening and I need a spin to shake off the office atmosphere before I see Jill. Thus David Hammond tried to justify why he had turned his car in the direction of Kensington. He stopped the car in front of Jill's flat. Julie's flat.

Jill was not at home. Jill was at his mother's house. Mary Hammond had quickly followed up her invitation to tea with a phone-call confirming the day. Today. David knew it. He was to pick Jill up there later. They were going out to dinner. That's why he was here.

He had talked to Julie several times on the telephone. Not deliberately. She always seemed to get to the phone before Jill did. Her very voice, husking its way down the wires, titillated him, angered him. Their exchanges were brief; they said nothing. Everything. Jill was worried about their relationship. She had complained privately to him that he was rude to Julie. She tried to get them to talk to each other when he went to the flat to pick her up. Julie smiled her enigmatic smile and ignored him.

He rang the bell, hoping she wouldn't be there, hoping that she would be. She opened the door. David hesitated, wondering how to explain his presence.

"Come in," she stood aside to let him pass.

"I thought you might be surprised to see me."

"Isn't Jill with your mother?"

"Yes."

"Then we both know where she is, don't we, and it's not here."

"You sound as though you were expecting me." David was annoyed. Julie held all the aces.

"If I knew a good bookie, I'd have won a bet." She was in trousers and shirt as usual. He wanted her. Hated himself for wanting her.

She poured drinks. Whisky. Neat. He didn't know how she

did it. She could drink him under the table. That's how she'd got him the last time, he justified himself. But he had to find out.

"Have you talked to Jill at all?" he asked, taking the glass.

"If we didn't converse now and then, sharing a flat would be as fatuous as your question, wouldn't it." She smiled mockingly at him.

He couldn't leave it alone. He had to know.

"About me."

"Believe it or not, you're not the sole topic of conversation between us." She looked at him. He looked unhappy. She felt sorry for him. "David, nothing important happened. Forget it."

He didn't want her sympathy. He didn't want Jill to know what had happened. But he didn't want Julie to think that what had happened was unimportant. Damn it, how dare she treat him in such an offhand way. As though he were just one in a line of men she had had. Women weren't supposed to behave like that. They came back begging for more. They didn't say tenderly that you should forget it, it was unimportant. Jill would be devastated if she knew. It was important.

"Jill was rather cross with me," he said.

"Why?" Julie didn't sound particularly interested.

"She thought I behaved as though I disliked you. I assured her that I did like you, deep down."

Julie laughed. "Deep down, you don't like me at all."

"No, perhaps I don't."

"Well, you do have a glimmer of self-perception after all."

"If I had the sense I was born with, I'd go, now."

"There's the door. You turn the handle and it opens inwards. It doesn't take much strength."

He hated her. He wanted to get up and walk straight out of this flat and never see her again. As she said, all he had to do was get up and do just that.

"You could always throw me out," he said.

"Oh, but you're so big and strong, David. I couldn't do that. Besides, I don't like you in exactly the same way that you don't like me."

He groaned, got up and took her in his arms. It was no use. He couldn't walk out now. He wanted her more than he had ever wanted anyone or anything in his life. But this would be the last time. After today, he would never see her again.

Their love-making was quick, violent, totally satisfying. He lay back exhausted but she wouldn't allow him to rest. He didn't think he could do it again but it was a challenge. The one time he felt in control was when she lay panting beneath him. Except this time, it was he who lay panting under her. Her arm was round his neck. He suddenly realised she was looking at her watch. Without a word, she got up. He watched her dress. He wanted to say something. Wanted to tell her that it wasn't unimportant. He couldn't find the words.

"Do you want a drink?" she asked casually as though addressing a stranger.

"No, I'd better go." He got up and started to hunt around for his clothes. Where were his cufflinks? He found one and put it in his pocket. He couldn't be bothered looking for the other.

"Yes, Jill's waiting, I expect."

"Yes, I expect she is."

"Well then, off you go. I'm going out anyway." Julie sat down at the dressing-table and started to brush her hair.

"You should have said. Before." David didn't like the idea of being used to while away an odd hour.

"I'm saying now." She looked at him in the mirror. "You're wishing you hadn't come, aren't you?"

"Yes," he said shortly.

"You always will. Every time."

"There may not be another time."

"That would be the most sensible thing, yes." Julie said agreeably.

"Yes. It would." Julie was taking the words out of his mouth.

"All right, fine. I'm not arguing."

He put on his jacket and stood uncertainly. He wasn't used to not being in control of the situation but here he was waiting for Julie to make the next move.

"Goodbye, David," she said.

He was dismissed.

He wasn't pleased to find Jill flanked by Brian and his mother. Tea had come and gone. They were drinking sherry. He apologised for his lateness but nobody appeared to have missed him. They were laughing and chaffing Jill as though she were one of the family.

It was Jill who suggested they give Brian a lift home. Brian invited them in for a drink. David wanted to get away. Go to eat in some anonymous restaurant with no connotations. But there was Brian confiding in Jill, telling her that Ann had left him. God, it had taken weeks before he'd told the family that. And there was Jill drooling sympathy, suggesting she cooked dinner here in Brian's kitchen. His protests were in vain. They ate their overcooked steak and Brian reacted as though Escoffier had spent the day preparing it. One cup of instant coffee and David stood up and announced it was time they were going.

Brian saw them to the door. "She's a really nice girl," he said to David.

David grunted. He felt trapped. This was how a performing animal must feel when the crowd clapped. The approval of the family was more than he could bear.

CHAPTER SIXTEEN

Brian had not felt so happy for a long time. He had taken out Pamela Graham several times and each time he liked her more. They had so much in common. Books. Music. She understood. And she cared what he thought and felt. She listened to him.

She was listening to him now. He had invited her back to the house for coffee after a particularly pleasant dinner. She had hesitated for a long time before accepting.

"Just for a minute," he urged. "I want to lend you that Ambrose Bierce book I told you about."

"All right." She had come in and stood by the living-room door while he hunted for the book for all the world like a small girl on the headmistress's mat, wondering when she was going to be allowed to leave.

"Pamela, will you sit down for a minute, please."

"It's quite late."

"Just for a moment."

Without removing her coat, she sat down, or rather perched, on the edge of an armchair. Brian looked at her. The moment had come.

"Pamela," he began. "I live in this house alone. That wasn't my choice in the first place. It was imposed on me. Am I supposed to lock the doors and keep everyone else out?"

"Do you want me to answer that now?" she asked slowly.

"No. It was a rhetorical question. It seems to me that I'm entitled to ask my friends to have coffee without everyone feeling uneasy about it."

"May I ask you something?"

"Yes, of course."

"Why did your wife leave you?"

It was a question that Brian had often asked himself but never been able to answer. He had half-asked Ann but her answers had never been satisfactory; they were airy-fairy, unrelated to reality.

"I don't know," he said. "I wish I could tell you."

"Surely you talked about it?" Pamela was incredulous. She

moved in a world where one analysed what one did and could explain every action. Ann was different. With her it was act now – and she didn't necessarily think about it later.

"We were never really able to talk," Brian explained. "Not the way you and I can talk. I'm sure there were faults on both sides. That's usually the case."

"Yes it is." Pamela was not being hard. She was looking at the situation objectively. Brian liked that. It made his thoughts important.

"I'm not a very demonstrative person, I suppose. I like an orderly life, a routine if you like. I'm a reasonably good provider. I enjoyed my children. I don't like emotional upsets. . . . and that may be part of the reason. Ann may need, oh, a kind of reassurance by way of rows and reconciliations and that I couldn't give her. I simply didn't like the rows. Anyway, in the end, I wasn't the right man for her, and that may well be a criticism of me. I know that." He stopped and looked at her. She seemed interested, sympathetic. But he didn't want to bore her with his dreary domestic troubles. He was enjoying just being a free man, alone with a pretty woman.

"Would you like some coffee?" he asked.

"Yes, I would. Thank you."

This was the sort of situation he had dreamed about. He sat sipping his coffee with a good brandy by his side and talked about books with someone who seemed to share the same tastes. They both liked French films so when he casually mentioned that the new Chabrol opened the following week, it was simple enough to follow up the announcement with an invitation. She looked beautiful in the soft light of the lamp. She was a peaceful person. That was the word. Peaceful.

The key grated in the lock. Brian froze. Pamela looked up enquiringly.

"Hullo, Brian." Ann swept into the room. She looked stunning as usual. This time in lilac suede with long, supple boots. She dazzled her teeth at Pamela. "Good evening, Miss Graham. How nice to see you again."

Brian and Pamela sat silent, stunned, unjustifiably guilty.

"Well," Ann sat down. "Would you get me a drink, Brian, please."

She leaned back proprietorially. "How's the school getting along, Miss Graham?"

"Very well, thank you, Mrs. Hammond."

"Carol often talks about you. To listen to her, one would think you knew everything. Perhaps you do, of course."

Pamela stood up. "I assume you came to talk to your husband, Mrs. Hammond, not me."

"I don't know." Ann took the glass from Brian's hand and smiled at them both. "Perhaps we could all talk about education in the broadest possible sense."

"Good night, Mrs. Hammond. Brian." Pamela didn't look at him.

"I'll see you to your car."

"Please don't bother."

"I'd rather if you don't mind." Brian was suddenly in control. He had recovered from his initial shock.

Ann seemed unperturbed. "I'll tell Carol that I saw you with her daddy, Miss Graham. She will be thrilled."

Ann had poured her second drink by the time Brian returned.

"That took a long time, darling." Ann looked amused. Brian was livid.

"There were some things I had to say."

"I can imagine."

"An apology was one."

"Whatever for?"

"Because she has every right to assume that if I invite her into this house, people are not going to come walking in unannounced."

"I'm not people. I'm your wife. And I have a right to come back to my own home whenever I want to."

"Did you have any reason? Apart from wanting to?"

"I needed to collect a dress. I thought I'd drop in. I'm sorry if I embarrassed you. I wasn't to know that you'd be enjoying a little tête-à-tête, was I?"

"I don't have to explain anything to you, Ann."

"Of course not, darling. If your inclinations run to the frozen spinster variety, that's your problem. Indulge it or get treatment for it. It's all the same to me."

"Ann, you are absolutely incredible." If he hadn't been so angry, Brian might have laughed. "I wasn't embarrassed. I was angry."

"I'm really not interested. I'll just go and get my dress." Ann made for the stairs but Brian stopped her.

"Let's get one or two things clear before you go. This house, which you didn't like, incidentally, ceased to be a family home the day you took the children and left. We're separated, Ann, and I have the right to make any friends I choose, without any comment whatsoever from you."

Ann was shaken. She hadn't expected Brian to react like this. Could he really fancy that dried-up little school-ma'am? The thought was preposterous. She liked Brian in this mood. He was masterful. Not his usual passive self. He hadn't finished.

"And don't ever come to this house again without asking me first. This is where I live, not you, and I may not feel like inviting you."

She made a step towards him then realised it was no use. Not tonight. She would go home now and think about her next step.

CHAPTER SEVENTEEN

While Ann was deciding on her plan of action, Brian was continuing to see Pamela. He felt quite pleased with himself. Ann had looked stricken the night he ordered her out of the house. He didn't think she would come back again without warning. The house still seemed very empty but he could live with that. He had the evenings to look forward to now. He had not invited Pamela back to the house since but felt it would happen all in good time. He didn't try to analyse his feelings for Pamela any more than he tried to analyse Ann's actions. He didn't really understand women. Ann was the only woman he had known well and he had taken her as his yardstick. Because of Ann, he saw the role of man as provider and protector. Marriage, to him, had meant submerging his own interest, the person he might have been, in order to be that unit demanded by society: the couple.

Pamela was different. She was an introspective young woman, used to analysing her own thoughts and feelings as she did those of her young pupils. Although not worldly, she had had one deep relationship with a man. It had left scars. It had left understanding. She knew this relationship could not drift on. Inevitably, it would have an ending. She wanted to be sure of what that ending would be. That way, you didn't get hurt.

She could talk to Brian about Ann and he quite enjoyed discussing his situation with her. He had been ashamed to admit to his family that Ann had left him. It seemed an admission of failure. But he never felt Pamela was judging him.

A few days went by before she broached the subject again.

"Have you seen your wife since?" There was no need to elaborate on the "since".

"No. There was a kind of flurry when she kept turning up all the time . . . I don't know why."

"Perhaps she isn't having quite such an interesting time as she thought she would."

"How do you mean?"

"Were you ever unfaithful to her?"

"No."

"I'm sure men find her very attractive."

"Yes, they do but if you're asking me . . ." Brian didn't go on. He didn't want to. Pamela understood that. What man would want to think of his wife having an affair. "I really don't know," he finished lamely.

Pamela tried to explain to Brian what she meant. She didn't think Ann was having an affair either but this was possibly not from choice.

"The attractive wife can go to parties on her own, or out to lunch, and have men around her and it's very easy and pleasant. As often as not, men are attracted to her just because she's safely married. But your wife is on her own now with two small children and a good many possible complications. Men don't like complications. She may find that boring."

Brian was surprised. "You sound very knowledgeable on the subject."

"I know her type, that's all."

Brian was even more surprised. He had never thought of Ann as a type.

"So what do you think she's doing?" he asked.

"She's clearing the decks for action. In case she decides that she wants you back after all."

It was an affront. "I might have something to say about that."

"I wonder if you will, once she makes up her mind."

Ann had not made up her mind yet. In the meantime, though, she was clearing the decks for the action she would decide on later. She was a Hammond if only by marriage. She decided to visit her family.

Edward was not particularly pleased to see her when she turned up in his office. He had never taken to Ann. If she was a type, she wasn't his, that was for sure. He always felt vaguely ill at ease with her. He tried to get her to see Brian but she insisted it was he she had come to see. When she started talking about the break-up of her marriage, he was embarrassed. He pointed out it was she who had walked out on Brian. Loyalty to Brian demanded at least that. She had looked unhappy, explained there was no other man, never had been, and left on a cloud of "My Sin".

Mary Hammond received her warmly. She longed for news of her grandchildren and she wished to stay friendly with Ann in case Brian would want her back one day. She had never regarded them as an ideal couple but Brian wasn't meant to live alone. He wasn't the type.

She was setting out nuts and crisps when Ann arrived. David was bringing Jill to dinner at her express invitation. It was a relationship she was at pains to foster.

Ann drained her glass. "I won't stay. I see you've got guests."

"David's bringing his girl friend to dinner."

Ann was interested. She had never known David do that before. "Is it serious?" she asked.

"I don't know. I'd like to think so but . . ." Mary suddenly felt she would like to talk to Ann about her hopes but David and Jill arrived just at that moment.

The introductions were made. Jill and Ann remembered each other vaguely from the Birkett party and started to chat animatedly. Jill because she was a sweet girl, disposed to like everyone; Ann, because if this girl were going to be a member of the family, wanted to have her on her side.

David groaned inwardly as Jill fished through her bag to find a telephone number of a marvellous little dressmaker for Ann. Wasn't there just one member of the family who wouldn't sweep Jill to their bosom? He felt vaguely jealous. Jealous and apprehensive.

Mary smiled on them all and insisted Ann stay for another drink. Everything was going so well lately. She had prevailed upon Edward even to bring Nancy Lincoln for a drink one evening. She was a pleasant woman. She refused to admit that she would find any woman who wasn't Jennifer Kingsley and who interested Edward pleasant. Her family was coming back to her. She felt needed. She felt in control.

Jill was relaxed, happy. She liked the Hammonds. She loved David. She wanted to marry him. She hadn't admitted it to herself but Julie had forced the admission from her. She had been amazed by Julie's reaction. Julie had seemed upset. She had begged her not to marry him because David was a nothing and she was too good for him. Julie had seemed so sincere. She hadn't been doing her usual hard bit. She had seemed genuinely to care. David handed Jill a glass and smiled at her. She smiled back and pushed thoughts of Julie to the back of her mind. She was happy. She would be lucky if David proposed.

Jennifer became more unhappy as the days went by. She couldn't get through to Barbara at all. When she had first heard that Nicholas Fox would be in France on business for some time, Jennifer had been pleased. Time for Barbara to forget him, to go around with boys of her own age. But then she had dropped her bombshell. She was going to Paris for a weekend to see him. Jennifer had remonstrated. Barbara had said flatly she was making her own arrangements, paying her own way. Jennifer might say it was a mistake. All right, but she had to make her own mistakes. Barbara couldn't see that Jennifer could not accept her arguments objectively. Couldn't see that she cared deeply. Barbara thought she was a woman. For Jennifer, she was her daughter whom she loved. And she was right to worry. Nicholas Fox had made it quite plain to Barbara that there was nothing in this relationship. He was relieved when Barbara insisted on paying for herself, not because he was mean but because it implied to him that she was equally independent. He didn't realise that behind the breezy exterior she had learned to adopt with him, Barbara was a complex of mixed feelings and emotions.

There was nobody in the dining-room. Jennifer played with the food on her plate, wondering what she could do about the situation. She was almost pleased to see Harry Carter. He helped himself to food and sat opposite her.

"What's wrong?" he went straight to the point. "Something's biting you."

"I'll get over it." Jennifer dismissed the subject but even Carter's casual concern warmed her, made her feel that the entire world wasn't against her.

"What you need is a night on the town. You know, a few drinks, a good dinner, go dancing."

"What I need is a few early nights."

"Wrong." Carter stabbed his fork in the air. "Take it from me, I'm an expert." Jennifer looked at him. What could this brash little man know about her feelings? He told her. "No one goes through a broken marriage and a love affair that went wrong without getting pretty depressed now and then. So I know what to do about it. I lay on a celebration and then I feel better."

Jennifer actually felt herself smiling. "Well, I suppose your method has one advantage. Whether you're feeling up or down, there's a party every night."

"Is there anything I can do, Jenny?"

"No, I'm all right."

"Well, if there is, just say the word."

"I feel better now anyway. I think I just needed someone who'd talk to me instead of at me."

"We could go out tonight."

"Not tonight. It would leave me fit for nothing in the morning. Are you one of those people who like staying up half the night?"

"I don't see what's so marvellous about sleeping your life away."

"Perhaps that's why you're usually late in at the office." She reprimanded him but gently.

Carter took it in good part. He knew what he was doing. "You want me to clock in with the drivers? Listen, I've done more than my fair share of that, I can tell you. Edward thinks he's achieving something by being there all the time, right? Well, I'm telling you. In a big organisation, if it can't run without you, you're not doing your job."

Carter took Jennifer's plate and his own and came back with two cups of coffee. He stirred sugar into his.

"I thought you and Edward had something going."

"No."

"Not any more, you mean."

"It's not something I want to talk about, if you don't mind."

"I don't mind. I just think it's healthy."

"Talking?"

"No. I mean it's healthy for the business. You're a clever woman, Jenny. You know what you're talking about provided you see things clearly and don't buy Edward's ideas nonstop."

"I never did that."

"Personal feelings can colour your opinions though. We see eye to eye a lot of the time, you and me. We could make that work for us."

Carter was pushing an advantage. He always did. At the same time, he genuinely liked Jenny. He found her attractive. She sensed this. It had been a long time since she had had any fun. She accepted his invitation to dinner that evening.

CHAPTER EIGHTEEN

Personal relationships were destined to be pushed firmly into the background. Hammond Transport was in trouble.

Edward's first inkling of it was when he took a telephone call from the bank. It was for Brian but Brian was lunching. At that very moment, he was in fact lingering over his third cup of coffee and discussing the pros and cons of Liszt with Miss Graham. His resultant euphoria was quickly dispelled when Edward greeted him with the news that he was to get over to the bank immediately and report back as soon as possible.

The report was bad. Hammonds were deeply in debt. The bank would not extend the firm's overdraft. Something had to be done and quickly. Brian would need a few days to draw up some proposals in time for the board meeting. Edward suggested they keep this between the two of them for the time being. Brian hesitated. He was responsible for finance. He would like the time to work something out. On the other hand, the other directors had a right to know what was going on. . . .

David found out they were in trouble when one of the firms with which he was drumming up new business telephoned to enquire about the delay in a quotation. Edward explained that no new contracts were being signed until after the board meeting. David didn't like it. He had an equal share in this company. He didn't see why Edward and Brian should be cooking up something between them. He was persuaded to wait for the board meeting. Brian was worried. He felt Edward had made a mistake in keeping quiet. It was Edward's first mistake.

By the day of the board meeting, Hammonds had been hit in other ways. Flu had spread through the depot and they were short of drivers. Deliveries to the Parker construction site had begun to fall behind schedule. Mortimer, Parker's man, came to see Edward.

"I had to come to see you, Mr. Hammond. It's getting desperate. We've got to do something. You promised me you'd keep to schedule but two loads due this morning haven't arrived yet. I passed them when I came in, just sitting there in the yard. Meantime, we're held up, men can't work, we get behind. Even Mr. Parker's worried. He must be, he sent me a cable."

"I'm very sorry and I'll get things moving right away." In his head, Edward was revising the schedule, wondering who he could get to do overtime. Riley would have to take a load out himself.

"I don't want to start talking about breach of contract, Mr. Hammond, but if we don't meet our completion date, we're in all sorts of trouble and what with everything else, I've got enough to sort out. We're working dead against the clock as it is and if our deliveries don't get through on time. . . ."

"I can see your problems, Mr. Mortimer, believe me," Edward cut in. "Hammond Transport will do everything in their power to keep the deliveries on schedule. All right?"

"They'll need to be, Mr. Hammond." Mortimer was like a determined terrier hanging on to a coat-tail.

"Right. I'm going to get those wagons moving right now." Edward stalked out of the room, leaving Mortimer to find his own way out.

Edward found Riley heading for one of the lorries. He had already decided to take it out himself. Two more drivers had reported sick. Edward watched the monster vehicle move away. The other stood silent, a threat to their very existence. There wasn't another driver on the site. He felt desperate. It was then he saw one of Carter's van-drivers getting out of his van. He had a sudden inspiration.

"Hey you!" he called. "Have you got a heavy goods licence?"

"Yeah!"

"What's your name?"

"Benson."

"Right. Get over to the traffic office and say you're taking the No. 2 lorry to the Parker construction site."

"Okay. Cheers." Benson walked off quite happily, thoughts of overtime pay large in his mind.

It was Edward's second mistake.

The board meeting began stormily. News that Hammond Transport was in serious financial trouble shocked Jennifer, Carter and David. They demanded to know why they had not been informed. Edward rapped on the table for the meeting to come to order. Brian continued his report.

"We extended ourselves in various directions as you know, acquiring Carter Express, the purchase of land, various other commitments . . ."

"We financed all those things," David interrupted him. "What's gone wrong?"

"We needed an additional working overdraft to see us through until our returns built up sufficiently to adequately cover our outgoings. The bank turned us down."

Carter went straight to the point. "So very soon, we run out of cash. No wages, no drivers, no lorries moving. We go bust."

"It's not as black as all that," Brian said. He was fighting to control himself. He was very upset by the state of affairs.

"You could have fooled me." Carter saw immediately just how black it was.

"We've got a breathing space," Brian explained. "The bank will meet us to some extent. We have to look for money, simple cash to keep operating from other sources. In the first place, our own clients. People who owe *us* money. We've got to get some of that money in fast. This is a detailed list of each customer, showing how much was owing to us up to the end of last week." He handed each of them a sheet of paper.

They digested the names and amounts in silence. It was Carter who spoke first.

"We're owed that much all told?" Brian nodded. "Get half that in and we're solvent."

"We'd not only be solvent, we'd be flush. But it's not that easy . . ."

Jennifer interrupted him. She had seen lists like this for twenty years. She had never seen such a list. "Brian, I'm sorry to raise this but we've never allowed this much credit before."

Brian felt uncomfortable. Jennifer was right. "I've carried out what amounts to an inquest over the last few days, Jenny. It is far too large."

"Why?" asked David.

"Since Dad died and we took over, we've expanded. The Borret contract, new business which you've been getting, David, now Carter Express. The accounting system has failed to cope with the additional business. Invoices sent out late, reminders not followed up. That sort of thing."

"Perhaps our accounting system should have been revised, Brian." David was furious.

Jennifer thought of Frank Walker and the system he had proposed. They had turned it down. Had they spoiled the ship for the proverbial ha'porth of tar?

"Or we should have modernised the system," she said.

"Let's not start a witch hunt," Edward hated post-mortems. They were a bloody waste of time. "We share the responsibility for this. All of us."

"Not me, mate," said Carter. "And I'd like someone to tell me how one firm can possibly owe us eighty thousand pounds?"

"Oh, that's Parkers," said Brian as though that explained everything.

"I can see it's Parkers. Eighty thousand grand? That's impossible."

Edward explained. "Tom Parker's our biggest customer. Has been for many years."

Carter was not impressed. "So what are we? His bankers as well?"

"With the amount of work we've been doing for him, plus the new contract of course – and we allow the normal three months credit . . ."

"This must represent more than three months credit, Brian," Jennifer asked.

Brian sighed. "I've already explained that our collection machinery doesn't function quite as well as it might."

"You mean that Parker not only owes us but he's not paying on time." Carter was incredulous.

"It'll be an oversight, that's all." Brian was actually not perturbed by the Parker debt.

Nor was Edward. "I'll have a word with Tom when he gets back. Let's look at some of the others. I reckon that if we can chase up about ten or twelve of the smaller fry. . . ."

What a typical limey way to do business. The old boys' act. Carter interrupted. "Why bother? All we've got to do is to get Parker to pay up and we're sitting pretty."

David was inclined to agree. "That would solve our problems in one. Do you think Tom would mind, Edward?"

"Who cares if he minds or not?" Carter again. "Tell him we need the money more than he does."

"We can't treat Tom like that," said Edward.

"Why not?"

"Yes, why not?" Jennifer was backing Carter now. She understood what he meant now about personal relationships being bad for business.

"He's an old friend of the family, that's why not," answered Edward. "If I talk to him tactfully, I'm sure he'll agree to help out."

Edward was talking about tact when the firm faced liquidation. "You tell us we need cash desperately," said Carter. "Right. He's got it. And he owes us."

"Tom was a friend of my father's, one of our first customers."

"I don't care if he's mates with the Archangel Gabriel."

Jennifer backed Carter again. "When a debt gets to eighty thousand pounds, it's time to stop talking about friendship. We're not here to lend Tom Parker money and that's what we're doing in effect."

They were all getting weary. Needling each other. Wrangling. Brian tried to put the voice of reason.

"This is ridiculous. You're talking as though Tom Parker's the villain of the piece. His credit is large because he's our biggest customer, that's all. The fact that he's always given us his business over the years has provided a foundation on which we can grow. He's on a normal, rolling credit. If we offend Tom Parker, we stand to lose more than we gain in the long run."

"In the long run, we're all dead," Carter spat out. "There's no room for sentiment in business."

"All right. All right," Edward brought the meeting to order again. "Let me try and sum up. Parker's on a cruise ship somewhere but I'll talk to him on the ship to shore line tonight. I'll tell him we need accelerated payment and try and reach some sort of agreement."

"And you'll report back to this board tomorrow." Edward glared at Carter. He was a nuisance. And he was trespassing on his, Edward's authority.

"I must have the authority to deal with Parker tonight."

"This board has the right to confirm or reject any deal you make," Carter challenged him.

Edward looked around the table. He wondered whether he could get the support of the others. Jenny? No. She'd taken

Carter's side pretty emphatically. Brian? Possibly. But he couldn't be sure. David? David was smarting still because of the new business he had lost and because he had not been informed of the trouble. Edward decided not to risk rebuff.

As they talked on about alternative ways and means, Edward suddenly became aware of a silence. The normal working background was the rumble of engines as lorries came and went into the depot. It had taken some time for the silence to impinge on his consciousness. He could hear only voices and the heavy tread of men's feet.

The men had stopped work. Benson was one of Carter's men. He was not a union member. Edward Hammond had promised that none of Carter's men would drive lorries. Yet he had ordered Benson to deliver a heavy load. He had broken his word. They had called a meeting.

Edward rushed over to the window. The others followed. They stared down at the scene below. In that instant, Edward realised what he had done. Realised there was nothing he could now do. Riley was bringing up the rear. He shut the gates behind him. For a moment, he looked up at the board-room window. He saw them all there but his expression didn't alter.

David remembered some words he had had with Riley earlier in the week. They had discussed the strike. He had pooh-poohed the idea of further trouble now that the union business had been sorted out. Riley had explained there was still a lot of ill-feeling. There could be trouble. David still hadn't understood. He thought everything had been solved. But Riley was adamant.

"Nothing was solved, Mr. Hammond. It was swept under the carpet out of sight and that's not the same thing."

David couldn't let it go at that. "If men are looking for a fight, Bill, they're liable to get it."

"I'd say there were some on your board of directors who wanted to take us on, Mr. Hammond."

David looked at his fellow-directors. He knew just who Riley was referring to.

CHAPTER NINETEEN

The fact that Edward had not been able to contact Tom Parker faded into insignificance. It was unimportant for the moment. The strike was on. Apart from being ordinarily crippling, the stoppage threatened the Hammonds' ability to fulfil the Parker contract which in turn threatened the completion date at the site. One thing led inexorably to another.

There was to be a meeting of the men that morning. But just now the depot was deserted. Lorries stood around where they had been abandoned by their drivers. The gates were closed. But clustered around them were a half a dozen drivers who were acting as pickets. It was a cold morning. The men stamped their feet and blew on their hands to keep them warm. A lone policeman watched them, hoping there would be no trouble. He touched his walkie-talkie radio for comfort.

Edward was the first to arrive. He had arranged a meeting with Riley and Reg Turner, the union organiser. He wanted to talk to them unofficially. The policeman straightened his shoulders as the car stopped. This could be the start of trouble. Edward leaned out of the car window.

"Open that gate," he bellowed.

Nobody moved. Nobody spoke. Edward got out of the car. The men stood aside to let him pass. The policeman relaxed visibly. Edward opened the gate. The pickets watched but nobody tried to stop him. He turned to the pickets.

"From now on, that stays open. Understand?"

Waters, the spokesman, shrugged. "All the same to us."

Edward got into his car and drove through. The pickets watched him go. No one attempted to close the gate again. Without speaking to each other, they formed a line across the entrance.

The incident happened a few minutes later. A Carter Express van tried to leave the depot. The driver was blaring his horn but the pickets gathered around the van didn't budge. They took the small van by the fenders and rocked and bounced it. The driver was no more than nineteen. He was trying to do his job. He was terrified. He kept his hand on the horn. The policeman could only watch. What was happening was on private property.

Edward arrived on the scene just as Carter's car pulled up. He had run from his office.

"Cut that out," he yelled, racing towards them.

Carter got out of his car and ran for the van. He ignored Edward.

"Get clear of that van," he ordered the pickets.

They didn't take any notice of him. They were enjoying themselves. They were in the position of power now. The young driver cowered inside. To them he represented what this was all about. He was a non-union man. He threatened their livelihood.

Nobody ignored Carter. He piled straight in. He grabbed one of the pickets by the arm.

"You, you ratbag. Get out of it!"

The picket swung round. Instinctively, he shaped up to Carter. Carter wasn't afraid. He was smaller than the other man, slighter, but he had had to learn to fight along the way.

"You try that, mate, and you'll finish up on your back."

The other man stopped. He glared at Carter for a moment in order to assess whether to take him or not. The other pickets had stopped rocking the van. They waited to see what would happen.

Edward stepped in. Automatically, they drew back. This was no Australian fly-by-night. He might be their enemy but he was a Hammond. "What's going on?" Edward asked.

Waters answered. "None of Carter's vans leave this depot."

"You want to bet?" said Carter.

"Calm down," Edward was in charge now. He opened the van door and the driver, terrified, got out. Edward turned to Waters. "You know the law and if not, it's time you learned it. Peaceful persuasion. Is that what you call this?"

He turned to the van driver. "Take that back to the loading bay."

The pickets were satisfied for the moment. Carter wasn't. This was bowing down with a vengeance. "Are you going to let that mob get away with it?"

"Anything like this happens again, I'm calling the law in." Edward turned away.

Carter followed close on his heels straight to Edward's office.

"Why don't you just hand the depot over to them and have done with it?" he stormed.

"Look, there are two ways to handle a strike."

"That's right. You win or you lose."

"We've had this conversation before."

Too right they had and Carter remembered the outcome. "Last time we did it your way. We buttered them up. Now look where it's got you."

"We do this by the book, Carter."

The two men glared at each other. Edward felt like thumping Carter. Carter wouldn't have minded. Both physical men, they would have preferred not to parry words. Sue, the new secretary, came in and announced Riley.

"Good," said Carter. "Let's see what he's got to say."

"I'll talk to him alone," Edward dismissed Carter.

Carter was suspicious. He didn't like these private deals the Hammond brothers seemed to spend all their time indulging in.

All anyone could do was wait. Jennifer and Carter had coffee together. David and Brian talked in Brian's office. Outside the gates, the men waited.

Edward and Riley talked. Edward laid it on the line. The depot was at a standstill. Loads were abandoned all over the country. There were contracts to meet. He asked Riley what the deal was.

"Get rid of the non-union men."

"Right," said Edward. "Carter's men. Eighty of them. Tell them they're fired. Put eighty men on the dole."

Riley looked at him. Edward had known what to say. Riley knew what it was like to be out of work. His father's stories of the Depression had made him a life-long socialist.

"It'll take a while to settle, Mr. Hammond. Let's not rush things. Reg Turner will be here soon."

They lined up in the board room. The Hammond Brothers, Harry Carter and Jennifer on one side of the table. Reg Turner and Bill Riley on the other. Edward opened the proceedings, explaining that the meeting was off the record since Turner was not yet representing the men outside but here at his invitation to talk things over informally before the position became too entrenched. Carter thought the whole thing a waste of time. If they weren't negotiating now, why not wait till the men had their meeting and proposals were made? Reg Turner explained patiently.

"If you want to wait for those proposals, that's up to you. But I ought to warn you that demands made in the emotional atmosphere of a mass meeting are likely to be tough. A number of old grievances are likely to emerge and they'll be included in those demands. Now, here's the point. Once the strike committee has been instructed to fight for those demands, they will have very little room to manoeuvre. And this strike could go on for months. Do I have to say any more?"

"No," said Brian. "Can we get on, Ted?"

Carter couldn't believe his ears. What was the Hammonds' attitude? He didn't know which side anyone was on any more.

Riley aired the men's grievance. It had been agreed that non-union drivers would not be allowed to drive heavy goods vehicles. Edward Hammond had yesterday instructed a van driver to take a heavy goods load to Parker's construction site. The men regarded this as a breach of faith.

While Edward explained he had been under pressure owing to sickness and hold-ups, Carter looked on contemptuously. He wouldn't carry on like this. Whose business was it anyway? And then Brian leaped in, all mealy-mouthed, to throw roses on the violets.

"This Parker contract means overtime for every driver in the depot. Virtually as much overtime as any man chooses to work. We were faced with a crisis situation. We're operating under penalty clauses."

Carter snorted.

"I know your problems," said Turner. "But it's almost ten o'clock. Does the management have anything positive I can put to the men or not?"

Edward chose his words carefully. "I'm prepared to give a personal guarantee that no non-union driver will be required to drive a heavy goods vehicle from this depot."

Turner shook his head. "Sorry, Mr. Hammond, but you said that before."

"I accept that, under pressure, I went back on my word and I'm prepared to go down to the meeting now and apologise."

Carter looked at Jennifer, amazed, and then at Edward. He must be off his head.

"Apologise!"

"That's what I said," Edward got up. "Let's get down there."

"Sorry, Mr. Hammond," said Riley. "It's a private meeting. Union card holders only."

They watched Turner and Riley leave the room in silence. Carter sat with his head slumped on to his chest in a stylised pose of despair which was not altogether insincere.

From time to time, they heard murmurings from the meeting. There was a burst of laughter at one point.

"Do I hear the sound of revelry?" asked David.

"Tell me when you hear the sound of lorries," said Brian.

"No chance," said Carter bitterly.

"You could be wrong," Brian pointed out.

"With Ted going down on his knees to them. What's he going to do for an encore – send 'em a bunch of flowers?"

Brian suddenly lost his temper. Edward was, after all, his brother and Carter an outsider.

"If this strike isn't settled," he stormed, "we lose the Parker contract and several others besides. Apologies cost nothing. Your way can put us out of business. Is that what you want? Because if not, stop knocking everything we do."

"He can't help it," David supported his brother. "It's the Australian national pastime."

"Gentlemen, I bow to your superior intelligence," Carter mocked them. "Now I know how you people lost your Empire."

"We didn't lose it. We gave it back."

They all glared at each other.

"All right, what's your solution, Carter?" Edward asked.

"Did I say I've got one?"

"You feel free to criticise mine."

"Only because I don't think it's going to work."

"You think you know my men better than I do?"

Carter did privately. "I didn't say that."

"Then why set out to antagonise them?"

"Look, just face up to the fact that you've got a fight on your hands."

"I think it's time you faced a few facts."

"All right," Carter agreed. "Let's have them."

"You are now working for Hammonds – at least theoretically."

"What do you mean 'theoretically'?"

"I mean that I doubt if you're putting in more than three hours a day at most. And I'm damned if I know what you do in those three hours."

"What do you want me to do – clock on?"

"Just pull your weight."

"Now listen. How do you think I built up my business? I've been working like a drover's dog since I was fourteen years old."

"And now you feel like a rest?"

"Are you being unfriendly, Ted?"

"That's what it's all about, isn't it? That's why you came in with us. You want to ride on a big animal."

"I reckon it's you that needs the rest, mate. Why don't you take a week out and come back when it's all over?"

Carter stalked out of the room. Brian got up and muttered something about making a telephone call. Jennifer followed him.

Edward moved to the window and stared down at the meeting as though willing them to make a decision to go back to work. David looked at him.

"How much do you trust Turner?"

"Rather more than I trust Carter."

David was surprised. "He's working for his members, Ted."

"He's also trying to hold down his job like everyone else. And his job is solving trouble not looking for it."

"I've been looking through the Act again," David picked up a copy from the table in front of him.

"Forget the Act. It's for lawyers' clerks. This is where you solve things. Face to face across the table."

"Then you're hopeful?"

"So long as they keep talking, I'm hopeful. I'll start worrying when they stop."

It seemed a long time before they did stop and the meeting re-convened. This time it was a negotiating meeting. The men had a list of proposals. Turner and Riley were accompanied by Waters and Nash who had been elected strike committee delegates.

Turner had been right. The emotional atmosphere of the meeting had resulted in a lot of demands. If Edward Hammond had been prepared to come down and apologise to the men, then they had him on the run. And they might as well get as much as they could from him.

There were nine proposals in all. They ranged from complaints about canteen facilities to the overnight boarding allowances. The matter of non-union drivers seemed to have been forgotten in the heat of the indignation generated by the state of the toilets. It was Turner who brought the meeting back to order.

"Let's stick to the main issues, shall we?" he said calmly. "We all have them in front of us. Nine principal areas of grievance . . ."

"But most of them are petty," David interjected.

"Of course, they're petty to you, son," Turner said kindly, but with a hint of patronage. "Because you don't have to cope with these problems day by day. Now let's try and deal with them in order. . . ."

Edward felt that control was slipping from him. It was Turner who was acting as though he were in the chair. He tried to regain authority.

"I'm sorry, Reg, but none of these complaints are what the strike is really about . . ."

As though on cue, Waters got to his feet. "Fair enough. Let's go."

"Hang on a minute, Jim," Turner indicated he should sit down again. "Let's have the management view."

The directors conferred briefly then made their proposal. Jennifer read it from her shorthand notes.

"Whilst the Board of Directors is prepared to give a written undertaking to the union that no non-union member shall again be instructed to drive a heavy goods vehicle . . . the other points raised subsequently by the men are not considered to be valid grounds for the continuation of the stoppage but may be discussed with the union later on, after the men return to work."

Waters was already on his feet and halfway out of the door. "Too late, darling," he called back over his shoulder. "Are you coming, Bill, or not? Just make up your mind where you stand."

Riley looked to Turner for guidance. Turner was already putting away his papers. It was the cue Riley wanted. He got up and followed Waters and Nash. Turner nodded at them all and left.

"God, what a waste of time," said Brian.

Edward didn't say anything. He had failed. He had conceded too much at the outset. That was his mistake. Carter had been right.

Edward brooded on the situation as he drove home. He was quiet throughout dinner which he ate with his mother. She looked at him from time to time but didn't say anything. He would tell her when he was ready. Edward was ready. He finished his cheese and glanced at the clock. It was a little late. Nine-thirty. But who could be bothered about the hour in this sort of crisis. He informed Mary he was having a meeting here at home. He went to telephone.

Mary was delighted. She liked to know what was going on. This made her feel part of the business. She bustled around checking drinks and cigarettes.

The people Edward summoned arrived one by one. Reg Turner. David. Brian. Bill Riley. Harry Carter and Jennifer arrived together. Jenny was dressed up. They had obviously been out together. Edward glowered at Carter. Mary beamed at Jennifer. She approved of the combination. The two people she most disliked – Harry Carter and Miss Kingsley. She complimented Jennifer on her dress and meant it.

Edward explained what he had in mind. He felt that there were a few things they could go along with. A new tea-urn for the van drivers to take some of the pressure off the canteen when the long-distance boys were arriving tired and hungry, for instance.

He also suggested that a committee be set up to thrash out all these points. Jennifer had been asked to take the minutes. She now re-read her shorthand.

"We propose that a joint consultative committee be set up consisting of two members of the management and two representatives from the drivers . . ."

"Heavy goods drivers," Bill Riley corrected her.

Carter didn't like that. "What about the van drivers?"

David thought that a fair point. He proposed that there should be three representatives on each side. These would include two lorry drivers and one van driver. Riley demurred.

"Not unless he holds a union ticket," he said.

"My drivers are entitled to representation," warned Carter.

"This is a union agreement," Turner said. "Your men don't come into it."

"And you think that's fair?" argued Carter, the outraged democrat.

It was becoming a philosophical discussion. Edward intervened. He pointed out that they had a working basis now. Management would sort out the other point between themselves. Jennifer would type the suggestions the following day and Turner and Riley would put them to the men at the next meeting. Turner and Riley left. Riley did not look very happy.

Carter was furious. "Well, wasn't that cosy. So now it's Hammonds ganging up with the union against my men."

"*Our* men, Carter," Edward said. "We're one company now. Try and remember that."

If it hadn't been for Carter, there wouldn't be this strike now. If it hadn't been for Carter, they wouldn't be up to their necks in money troubles. Money. They hadn't been able to get hold of Tom Parker. His mother had insisted that Tom wouldn't let them down but Edward felt uneasy. It was strange that Tom should go off on a Mediterranean cruise when he'd landed a big council contract. Carter had voiced his own suspicions. Suppose Carter were right?

CHAPTER TWENTY

When Edward's telephone call had come, summoning him to the extraordinary meeting, Brian had been comfortably settled in front of the television set with Pamela Graham. They had had an early meal in order to get home in time to see a documentary which interested them both. Brian thought fast. He suggested that Pamela should stay on and watch. She agreed, saying she would lock the door behind her when she left. Brian was a little disappointed by that. He half-hoped she would wait for him. It would be nice to come home to someone waiting.

It had been late when he got back. The lamp was still burning. He was surprised and delighted. From the door, all he could see was a figure stretched out on the settee. She had stayed.

"Pamela," he went towards her. "I'd hoped you might . . ."

The figure stirred and sat up. It was Ann.

Waiting for Pamela here in the bar where they had arranged to meet, Brian's blood ran cold, remembering. Ann had been as unperturbed as always. She told him she had had a nice little chat with Miss Graham. God knows what she had said. He hadn't waited to find out. He had spent the night in an hotel.

Pamela Graham had been shocked at first by Ann's appearance. She had scrambled to her feet intending to go but Ann had insisted she stay. They had had a drink or two together. Pamela was not always so perceptive as she fondly imagined. Ann had been very clever. She had talked about Carol, explained how worried she was about her. She intended Miss Graham to feel sorry for her and she had succeeded.

Then Ann had brought the conversation round to Brian. She asked Miss Graham whether she didn't find his excessive tidiness an irritation. Pamela had stammered that she didn't know him that well.

"It probably hasn't registered too much as yet," Ann said casually. "People are always on their best behaviour at the beginning of an affair."

"There isn't an affair," Pamela said hotly.

"I did say – the beginning." Ann was being very subtle.

"Not even a beginning."

"How many of us ever admit that to ourselves until it's too late?"

Ann had made her point. She had crystallised what Pamela herself had been thinking. There were only two ways for her relationship with Brian to end. It was probably best if she ended it before it was too late.

Brian looked tired and rather worried. Her heart warmed as she saw him. He never actually looked relaxed until she had arrived, as though he were always expecting she wouldn't turn up.

"I had some marking to do, sorry."

"Not at all." He sounded relieved. "I'm surprised you were prepared even to see me again after last night. Was it very embarrassing?"

"At the beginning but then quite, well, fascinating really."

"In what way?" Brian stared at her.

She didn't answer for a moment. "You and Ann are an odd combination," she said finally.

"You've met her before."

"She has different facets."

"Don't we all?"

"No, you don't. I don't think I do."

"Moods?"

"Not the same thing. Ann can change completely in the space of a few seconds. It must be very disconcerting."

"It is." Brian wasn't sure whether he wanted to talk about this any more. He signalled the waiter.

"What facet was she displaying last night?" he asked.

"She wants me to bring you two together."

It was impossible. "She said that?"

"No. But she meant that."

"She left *me*." He spelled it out for her.

"Is that important?"

"It's a fact."

"Or a convenient excuse."

Pamela seemed to be on Ann's side. "She did a good job on you," he shrugged.

"That's insulting."

"I'm sorry." He was.

"Did you drive her out?"
"Good God, no."
"Not even subconsciously?"
"Do you think I wanted to lose the children?"
"But you admit wanting to lose Ann?" It was an interrogation.
"No, I don't," he said vehemently.
"In that case, you can have no objection to having her back."
So that was female logic in operation. Just like Ann. They were all sisters under the skin. He signalled for the waiter to bring a fresh round of drinks.
"I think you should stay sober," Pamela said. She sounded like a bloody schoolteacher.
"Why?" he asked.
"Because there are a few things I think we should straighten out. So far we've avoided them."
"All right." Brian knew it was true. They couldn't go on like this. He knew they would have to discuss the situation sometime.
"Last night, Ann accused me of having an affair with you." She hesitated.
"That's typical."
"I said that you didn't interest me."
"Oh." Brian was rather disappointed.
"That wasn't strictly true." He felt better already. "Neither is it true that we're having an affair. But she was right on one thing. If we go on seeing one another, that's exactly what could happen. Is that what you want?"
"*If* it happens . . ." Brian was being cautious but Pamela was determined to talk this through.
"Just face the issue," she said crisply.
"Yes, I suppose it is now. But it didn't start off that way."
"Brian, I don't want it to go any further."
Suddenly, he did. He had faced the facts at last. Now it was his turn to put the questions.
"Don't want to? Or feel you shouldn't?"
"I am not going to break up your marriage."
"It's broken . . ." He realised that now.
"Not beyond repair. So can we agree to call things off right now?"

She was asking him, not telling him. He thought for a moment.

"And what about my feelings?"

"I don't know what they are," she said.

He paused only for a moment. "I think I'm in love with you."

He signalled the waiter again. This time she didn't stop him.

David had hoped to relax with Jill. The troubles at the depot made him look forward to some gentle company. He supposed it was why men got married. When he didn't have a regular job, he enjoyed the challenge and stimulus of a variety of girl-friends of different humours. But work now gave him all the challenge and stimulus he needed. He conveniently forgot about Julie.

Jill turned up at his office that afternoon. She had had bad news. She had just heard that her father had died and she was going to the country for the funeral. It was all a big rush. She hadn't seen her father very often since he and her mother had divorced but she was upset. She had been fond of him. She had had an unsettled family background and she felt she had missed out on something important. She tried to explain this to David.

"It's happening more and more these days," he said.

"It always did. Amongst those who could afford it."

He looked at her fur jacket and expensive trousers. "So what do you do? Induce a state of poverty to preserve the marriage?"

Although nothing specific was said, they were probing about their own future. Each wanted to know where the other stood.

"No, David. You make sure you marry the right person in the first place."

"How do you do that?"

"I don't know. Instinct, I suppose."

"But people change . . ." David was resisting the idea.

"They can change together."

"Get bored with each other . . ."

Jill wanted to know suddenly. "If they're the kind of people who get bored easily, then they'll just get bored with someone else. So what have they gained?"

"This is a silly conversation," David laughed. "Neither of us have been married, so neither of us know."

"There may be some virtue in innocence."

"That almost sounds as though you're proposing to me," David's voice was deliberately casual.

"That's a man's job. . . ."

David side-stepped the situation. "Do you have to go tonight? I'll miss you."

She kissed him. "That's good. But you can survive one evenig. Oh, by the way, David, if I give you the key, would you feed the cat for me?"

"Why can't Julie do it?"

"She's going to Birmingham tonight. On location."

"Oh. All right. I'll do it." A flicker of disappointment spread over his face for a moment which he quickly concealed. If Jill saw it, she didn't say anything. She just smiled and thanked him.

Feeding an already overfed cat was not his idea of a jolly evening. David got out the tin-opener and attacked the can viciously.

"Now there's a happy, domestic scene. You'll never starve."

"What the. . . ." He whirled round. Julie leaned on the kitchen door smiling at him.

"I thought you were in Birmingham."

"I got out of it."

"Jill's gone to . . ." It was gratuitous information. Julie mocked him with her eyes.

"I know. For the night."

He spooned the meat onto the plate. The cat came running, purring and rubbing against him. Julie turned to go.

"I'll fix us a drink. And there's steak if you're hungry."

"I didn't say I was stopping."

"You didn't have to."

She was right. He stayed. He had a drink and he had a steak. All the time he told himself he was doing it for a reason. He was going to have a civilised evening with Julie. Put things back on the right footing. Square things with his conscience. He offered to wash up.

"Don't worry. Jill will do it tomorrow."

"I can't imagine why she shares a flat with you."

"It's her social work, darling."

"Well, I'll be off then." David got up. He was suddenly very unsure of himself. All his good intentions were evaporating. Julie was off-hand as ever.

"As you always say."

"This time I intend to."

"All right. Goodbye."

"Goodnight, Julie." He moved towards the door.

"Just so that I have time to look round for something suitable, when's the wedding?"

"I didn't know there was going to be one."

"Oh well, I expect someone will get round to telling you eventually. Probably Mummy as you're halfway down the aisle."

"Did Jill say we were . . . ?" David thought he saw the drift of Jill's conversation that afternoon.

"She doesn't have to. She's just gone broody."

"And what signs do you see in me?"

"The sudden onset of guilt."

David hesitated. He should have turned then and gone. But he stepped back to confront Julie. It was a fateful step.

"Don't you ever feel mean, cheating on your best friend?"

"The incredible hypocrisy of the man!" Julie roared with laughter.

"Or does she know already?" David was worried and Julie knew it. She made capital of it.

"Now that's something that could intrigue you for a while, isn't it. Are you going to open another bottle of wine or just stand there like a naughty boy?"

He looked at her. He knew what attracted him to her. She did just what she wanted and didn't give a damn. He pretended to be like that. He'd been one of the Chelsea tearabouts. But everything he'd done had been because it was trendy, the thing to do whether you liked it or not. He stepped towards her and took the corkscrew from her. There was time for another glass of wine. Jill was away for the night.

CHAPTER TWENTY-ONE

There had been an unpleasant scene in Jennifer's office the day she had prepared the proposals for submission to the strike committee. The directors had arrived early to read and ratify the suggestions. The directors except for Carter. Jennifer had wanted to wait for him but Edward would not allow it. She explained that Carter wanted to talk to his own men and then put some alternative suggestions.

Edward was not interested in Carter's alternatives. If he had any worth hearing, he should have turned up on time to offer them. And he didn't like Jenny knowing things about Carter's movements. They must obviously have spent time together the previous evening.

"He's on the Board," Jennifer insisted. "You cannot just ignore him."

"Carter caused this strike."

Jennifer was appalled by Edward's unfairness. "He didn't cause it. We did by buying him up."

"That's past history. Anyway, just because you fancy him . . ."

"Don't be ridiculous."

"Then what were you doing with him last night?"

"How dare you!" Jennifer was furious. It was all right for him to go around with this Lincoln woman but she was supposed to stay at home brooding, was she? "I can go where the hell I please!"

They were screaming at each other. Neither of them really cared what they were saying any more. To any student of human nature, their abandon, the vituperative insults, were sure signs that they still cared about each other, although both would have succumbed to torture rather than admit it.

"What do you see in him, for God's sake? He's vulgar, vain, crass. He's a bore . . ."

"He's a man who can stand on his own feet."

"Anchored in concrete."

"At least he built up his own business. He didn't have it handed to him on a plate by his father!"

"And what did my father hand you on a plate?"

The blow went home. Jennifer tried, weakly, to parry it.

"Nothing I didn't work for."

"Damn right you worked for it." Edward spoke in anger, in jealousy, but what he said was unforgiveable.

Jennifer screamed at him to get out of her office. She was almost hysterical. She kept repeating "Get out! Get out!" Edward became alarmed suddenly. He grabbed her and told her to be quiet. For a brief moment, he wanted to draw her towards him, apologise. But Jennifer spoiled it. She lowered her voice but it only gave more weight to what she said.

"You're jealous, aren't you. Jealous of Harry Carter. The man you pretend to despise."

"I don't despise him." Edward suddenly marshalled his attitudes towards Carter and what he said was true. He had a lot in common with Carter. "I just think Carter's doing us harm. And I wish to God there was some way of getting shot of him."

"Well, it's too late. You're stuck with him," Jenny gloated.

"Have I come at a bad moment?" Carter's head appeared round the door.

"You're the bad moment," Edward turned on his heel. He paused and looked back at Jennifer. "And I'll tell you something else about Harry Carter. Not only is he vulgar, vain and crass, he's bone idle."

Carter grinned. "I thought he was going to say something bad."

There wasn't much to do in the office that day. Traffic movement sheets were drawn up – more in hope than anything else. Telephone calls were made to every conceivable place where Tom Parker might be. All to no avail. It was a long day.

The next morning, work was undertaken more cheerfully. They would hear soon whether the suggestions had been adopted by the committee. They were fair proposals. They were hopeful.

The committee turned the proposals down. Riley explained that they were not in the mood for compromise proposals. What they wanted was to get rid of Carter and his non-union drivers. Edward would have liked that, too. But, as Jennifer had said, he was stuck with them.

"You're not talking for the men," he pointed out.

"No. The committee will put the proposals to them tomorrow at the mass meeting. But with the recommendation that they're rejected."

Tomorrow. Another day to wait. Another day behind on schedules. Another day in which debts would mount up and goodwill would diminish. And even then, it seemed probable the men would vote to continue the strike. Reg Turner had told them about one strike that went on for three years.

Edward's assessment of Carter had not been altogether correct. Vulgar and crass he was, in many ways. To some people he was a bore. But then everybody bores somebody; it's all a question of taste. Bone idle, he wasn't. True, he believed in what is sometimes called delegation, sometimes skiving, depending from where you view it. But he could snap into action fast when necessary.

His fellow directors at Hammonds had not waited to hear his suggestions. It was just as well in the circumstances. The strike committee would probably have thrown them out along with the others. Now they were a card up his sleeve. He had derived a certain amount of pleasure from watching Edward Hammond in the role of stag at bay. But it was time to end the strike now. Time for Harry Carter to put in his three hours' work a day.

The meeting took place at his penthouse flat. Carter had selected his guests. Edward, Jennifer, Reg Turner and Bill Riley were all he needed. After drinks had been dispensed, he got down to business. He crystallised the problem for them: the main stumbling-block to the solution of all problems was one Harry Carter. He had a plan which would get Harry Carter out of their hair.

The men were beginning to quieten down ready for the meeting when Harry Carter and Edward Hammond arrived. There were a few cat-calls and jeers as they approached. This was no place for bosses. Waters brought them to order. He was as much in the dark as they were.

"I'd just like to say," he began, "that there have been certain developments in the past twenty-four hours which I think it would be better if Reg here told you about. After that, we shall be having a vote."

Reg Turner stepped forward: "It has been agreed by the strike committe that we should invite Mr. Edward Hammond and Mr. Carter to be present for the first part of this meeting and Mr. Carter would like to say a few words."

There were a few boos and requests, indelicately phrased, that Carter and Hammond should be on their way. Harry Carter came forward jauntily and grinned round at them all. He knew how to handle men.

"Brother Chairman, fellow workers . . ." he said.

The jeers got louder. Turner raised his hand for silence.

"Give him a chance, please . . ."

Carter kept on smiling. Edward repressed the hope that he would be shouted down.

"That's all right," Carter laughed. "I like a bit of opposition and I appreciate a good fight. But then perhaps I'm just a rough Aussie. But it's been a good fight, fought clean . . . and you've won."

The men were silent now. Listening.

"So, well done, lads. I've been a driver for twelve years."

"A non-union driver," a voice at the back called.

"That's right. Until last night. I now have an application form from Reg here to join your union."

"You're a boss!" It was the same voice.

"Oh no," Carter smiled at them all, confidingly. "I am an employee of Hammonds, the same as you are. And Reg agrees with me that it's only right and proper that I should join your union. Twelve of my van drivers have agreed to follow my example. Perhaps you'd like to take care of them, Reg."

There was a stunned silence followed by a spontaneous burst of clapping. Waters was amazed. This wasn't what he had wanted. He was looking forward to the strike. He was anti-boss on principle. This was to have been his big moment.

Reg Turner took from Carter the sheaf of union application forms. He looked round the men.

"I have a proposal from Bill Riley, seconded by Bob Nash, for an immediate resumption of work. All those in favour, please show."

All hands went up, even Waters', although his was the last.

Harry Carter satisfied himself that the vote had been carried then walked towards the iron staircase and the office.

Edward watched him go. Carter had won the day. It had been nicely timed, nicely planned. It was the first step towards the chair.

CHAPTER TWENTY-TWO

The strike over but the financial troubles lingered on. The bank would not grant Hammonds another penny on their overdraft. Tom Parker had still not surfaced. Mortimer, his second-in-command, was not empowered to make payments.

To cut off deliveries to the Parker site would not solve their problems. If Hammonds did that, Parker would lose the council contract. The moment that happened, Parker's creditors would move in and force him into bankruptcy. Hammonds stood to end up with ten pence of every pound that Parker owed them. The only thing they could do was continue supplies.

Carter had told them all this days ago yet Edward was still insisting that Parker was on old family friend, that they had to trust him. He felt it was Mortimer who was mismanaging things. Jennifer was uneasy. There was too much talk of friendship.

It was David who wondered why Parker had not come back to sort out Mortimer's mismanagement. Edward had to admit he had no answer. Parker had last been heard of in Yugoslavia. It was suggested that someone should fly out to contact him. David volunteered. He liked Yugoslavia. But it was Edward who was elected for the task.

It would be a wild-goose chase. Edward didn't want to go. He didn't know where to start looking. Yugoslavia! It was a pretty big country. Even if Parker were still there. And he was afraid he wouldn't be. He now knew although he wouldn't admit it that Parker had welshed on the contract. Bad enough when anyone did it. But an old friend of the family. He wished he didn't have to go.

Another reason Edward didn't want to go was that he was nervous. He had never in his life been abroad by himself before. It had been eight years since he had taken a holiday. That had been in Clacton. He had gone by car and come back two days later. He didn't like holidays. He didn't like abroad. He wished he didn't have to go alone.

He invited Nancy Lincoln to go with him. She prevaricated.

"I have a job to do."

"Would they miss you for a few days?"

"Probably not," she said frankly.

"Then why don't we?"

"My husband's ill."

"So? You're separated."

"That doesn't stop me worrying about him. He needs looking after."

"How long have you been looking after him?"

"I've always looked after him even though we don't live together."

"I knew you went to see him occasionally but I didn't know there was any more to it than that."

It was the wrong time but the right moment. Nancy had to sort out this situation now. "What did you think?" she asked slowly.

"Well, I assumed you were heading for a divorce or something."

"Did I ever say that?"

Edward thought for a moment. "No, that's true."

"There is still a certain dependency."

"You mean he depends on you to bail him out whenever he gets drunk. What's the future in that?"

"I don't know," she shrugged.

"I don't want to go on this damn trip on my own," Edward returned to his own troubles.

"Isn't there anyone from the firm you can take with you?"

"Such as?"

"I don't know them, do I. But what about Jennifer Kingsley?"

"No." He spat it out.

"Wasn't there something between you two?"

"Not any more."

"That's a shame."

"You think so?"

"Yes, if it makes you more dependent on me. I don't think I could cope with two dependent men."

She was telling him something. Edward knew that. He asked her straight out,

"Are you trying to get rid of me, Nancy?"

"Of course not," she kissed him lightly on the cheek. "Have a good trip, Edward, and call me when you get back."

She was lying. He knew it. Nobody was on his side any longer.

Experience of death tends to make one more conscious of life. It becomes important to use time rather than just drift along. When Jill returned from her father's funeral, she knew it was time to find out whether or not David loved her. They could drift on forever otherwise.

Mary Hammond was entirely disposed to helping along the operation. David had put off telephoning Jill all day. He felt guilty. He felt resentful, too. His entire family seemed to be manoeuvring him to the altar. And he lusted after Julie. He hated the idea of any woman's haunting him the way that Julie did but she did. He found himself thinking of her in unlikely moments – in board meetings, for instance. The last time had been incredible again. It was as though they could never get enough of each other. Nothing seemed wrong. They enjoyed each other in every possible way. He put off telephoning Jill because it was Julie he wanted to talk to. Julie's voice he wanted to hear. And he was afraid. Afraid that Jill might find out.

"I really think you should call Jill," his mother said. "She will need comforting and if you leave it too long, she will find comfort somewhere else."

"Who – Jill?" David was surprised. Jill he took for granted. She was there when he needed her. Like a wife.

"Don't sound so surprised. She's a very attractive girl. You don't imagine she's going to hang around waiting for you all her life, surely."

It was an unpleasant thought. David reacted as his mother had intended. He arranged to meet Jill at his flat. They decided to eat in.

"I fed the cat," said David, seeking praise and information.

"And Julie as well, I hear."

"Did she tell you?"

"There are no secrets between us." Jill looked at him closely.

David bustled around getting drinks.

Jill came up behind him. "Do you like her any more now that you know her better?"

"I don't know how you put up with her." David could say that and mean it.

"She's amusing. She has a marvellous fund of gossip."

David didn't like the sound of that. Was Jill leading up to something?

She was. "Darling, did you stay with Julie last night?"

David was outraged as only the guilty can be. How dare Julie betray him! "Is that what she told you?"

"No."

"Then why accuse me of it?"

"I didn't. I just asked you."

"If she's trying to mix it between you and me . . ." David threatened.

"She isn't. And you haven't answered."

"No, I didn't spend the night," he lied.

"I've no right to stop you." David did not react to this. She went on. "I just like to be told the truth. It's important that we should be able to tell the truth to each other, isn't it?"

David still didn't answer.

"Only you left a cuff-link in the bathroom." She took a cuff-link from her handbag and handed it to him.

He took it, thinking fast. "I washed my hands after feeding the cat."

"Yes, of course." Jill smiled at him. She didn't believe him. But at least she had established that she was important enough to him for him to lie to her.

Jill decided not to be available for a few days. She wanted David to have time to think. The next time he called, Julie informed him Jill was in Pontefract. She hadn't left a number. He rang off quickly before he responded to the open invitation in her voice.

He found himself thinking about Jill. He missed her. She was sweet. Lovable. He had finished with her once. A year later, he had met her again and found her as attractive as ever. If he gave her up again, it would be the last time. He had his second chance now. There wouldn't be a third.

He cross-questioned Brian about marriage. His brother wasn't particularly helpful. Marriage was not a subject on which he now considered himself an expert. He did say, though, that Jill was very sweet. Lovable.

What would he do if he let her go again? Go out with Julie?

That wouldn't last long. Anyway, part of Julie's attraction lay in the danger of the situation. Look around for someone else? He was getting older. He was getting past that Chelsea stage. It was doubtful he would find anyone so suitable as Jill again. Suitable. An odd word to crop up when thinking about love. But, then, David didn't know whether or not he was in love.

There was something else, too. Maybe it was his mother's remarks, maybe just nature demanding her due, but David felt he would like children. He didn't particularly like children. He didn't know any except for Brian's and he never found much to say to them. But children were a continuation. They satisfied that need for immortality for those whose work is not destined to live forever.

It was David's first intimation of mortality which made up his mind. It happened the day of Jill's return. He had arranged to meet her for dinner that evening. He was surprised at how pleased he had been to hear her voice. Bill Riley came in as he was murmuring endearments down the line at her.

There had been an accident. One of the drivers had been trapped in his cab. They had had to cut him out. He was dead on arrival at the hospital. David didn't know what one did in such situations. Riley explained that Edward usually called in person. Edward was not here. David went with Riley.

The widow received them. She was quiet, broken; impressed and overwhelmed by the presence of a Hammond in her tiny living-room. She had listened in silence to their painful news then thanked them for coming.

David cried as he told Jill about it. She held him close and stroked his hair. She felt so warm. He clung to her. He knew now what he needed. He wanted a defence against the pains and miseries of the world. He needed someone. He asked her if she would marry him. She nodded.

He broke away for a moment and looked at her. "Would you?"

"Yes," she said.

Pamela Graham had thought a lot about Brian. He had told her he loved her. She knew he had meant it when he said it. But he wasn't the sort of man who could cheerfully go from one woman to the next. Ann had said he was excessively tidy. Tidiness for him was emotional as well as physical. He wouldn't care to have an ex-wife and ex-children floating around. Ann and Brian were very different people but they had been together for years. They had a lot in common. Perhaps they only took different routes to the same solution?

They sat in Brian's living-room. She refused a drink. What would these people do without alcohol, she thought? Confronted with any situation, they reached for a bottle. She made Brian feel guilty. As he poured himself a large whisky, he tried to make a joke.

"I'm one of those people who are always one drink under."

"Then you'll end up an alcoholic."

Brian was angry. "Why are you giving me a hard time?"

"Because you gave me a hard time. You said you loved me and I was flattered. That was my initial reaction. But then I was forced to examine what I thought about *you*."

"And concluded?" Brian took a nervous swallow of his drink.

"That I'm being used."

"By me?"

"By both you and your wife. As a pawn in your love-hate game. That's not for me, Brian. You've found the wrong woman."

She stood up. "I've brought your books back. I hate people who never return books they borrow."

"Look," Brian wanted desperately to keep her there. He didn't want it to end like this. "Look, just have a drink, would you?"

It wasn't what she had come to hear. "No, thanks, really. I just came to say goodbye."

"I'd like to stay friends."

"Of course."

Brian couldn't believe it was ending like this with an exchange of platitudes. "Pamela – what have I done?" he asked plaintively.

"Nothing. It's me. I'm in the way."

"Ann isn't coming back."

"I think she is."

"I'm not having her back."

"You are."

"How can you say that with such total conviction?"

She didn't answer. "I really mustn't stop," she said.

He took her in his arms. She didn't try to pull away.

"Pamela," he whispered, burying his face in her hair. "Don't go, Pamela. I need you."

She pulled away then.

"No. I've served my purpose. Goodbye."

She walked towards the door. Brian watched her go. If he had gone after her at that moment, stopped her, told her he loved her . . . He didn't. She had made the decision. He accepted it.

He looked at the books she had brought back. They were his favourites. They had spent happy times discussing them. He put them back on the bookshelves in their right places.

Barbara's weekend in Paris had been a disappointment. Her French was not good, which made getting around by herself difficult. She hadn't expected to be by herself so often. She had thought Nicholas would have devoted the weekend to her. But he was busy. She had dutifully tramped round the Louvre, the Jeu de Paume and the other artistic delights of Paris, meeting Nicholas at pre-ordained times for coffees and cognacs. They had had dinner both nights with friends of Nicholas. The friends had turned out to be business colleagues. Nicholas was thinking of taking a job.

There was an advertising conference in Paris that week. One of the agencies wanted Nicholas to work for them. Barbara couldn't believe it.

"Doing what?"

"They want me to run their Art Department."

"But you're an artist."

"That's why they want me to run their Art Department."

"But you're not a commercial artist?"

"God, you students are all the same. There's nothing wrong in being commercial."

Barbara was disappointed. Art, bohemian life, Left Bank idealism. She had thought they were all summed up in Nicholas Fox.

"I thought you were different," she accused him.

"I'm sorry to shatter your high principles but that's the way the cookie crumbles." Nicholas stubbed out his cigarette. The job would pay very well. Better than being visiting lecturer to an art school and slogging your guts out preparing for exhibitions at which you might sell four paintings if you were lucky. It had been a mistake to suggest Barbara came here. She was wet behind the ears. She wasn't out for a good time at all. He was sick of her face looking at him with those reproachful eyes. Anyone would think he had just announced that he had decided to take up cannibalism or painting by numbers or something equally obscene.

"If you can bear to eat an excellent dinner tonight paid for by the profits from the exploitation of the masses via advertising, we're invited to the Tour d'Argent."

"No. No." Barbara hesitated for a moment then made up her mind. "I've decided to go back early. I thought I'd get the seven o'clock plane."

"When will I see you then?"

"Back in London, I expect. Goodbye Nicholas. Thanks for. . . ."

"Everything?" he forced her to finish the cliché.

She was made of sterner stuff.

"Thanks for the nice things."

She got up and hurried away. Nicholas stared after her. He hadn't expected that. She was an interesting little thing. That ability to surprise him. He liked that. So what? There were a thousand Barbaras around. He shrugged and ordered another cognac.

CHAPTER TWENTY-THREE

While Edward was away, Harry Carter took the second step to oust him as chairman of the Board of Hammonds.

The step was motivated by two things: ambition, and the news that before he had left for Yugoslavia, Edward had made him warehouse manager.

Harry went straight to Jennifer's office. She confirmed that he had indeed been made warehouse manager at the board meeting which he had not been able to attend. David had suggested rather unpleasantly that the reason for Carter's absence was that Millwall was playing at home.

"I take it Ted's halfway across Europe by now," asked Harry.

"I would think so."

"That's a shame. I was just about to tell him what to do with his warehouse. Can I see the minutes of that meeting?"

Jennifer handed them to him. He scrutinised them for a moment. He saw that Jennifer had not voted with the Hammonds. His hunch had been right.

"I'm going to be blunt with you, Jenny," he said. "Ted's made two very bad errors recently. One landed us with a strike. The second could put us into bankruptcy."

"Neither can be laid entirely at his door."

"The man in charge takes the rap. That's the first law of business. We've got a real cow of a problem on our hands . . ."

Jennifer shrugged. "Have that out with him when he comes back."

"I don't think we can wait that long. Since you're all so keen on board meetings, I'd like to call one."

"Only the chairman can call a board meeting."

"Where does it say that?"

"In the articles of association."

"It doesn't," Carter chortled. "I read them again this morning. In the case of an emergency and when the Chairman is absent, a Board Meeting may be called with the mutual consent of the remaining directors."

"Do you have their consent?" Jennifer wanted to know.

"Let's start with you."

"I'd want to know what this meeting is for."

"A decision was made in my absence to make me warehouse manager. I want that decision reversed. That's point one." He stopped.

"And point two?"

"I want to propose a new chairman for Hammond Transport."

Jennifer paused. "Yourself?"

"No. You." Carter smiled at her surprise.

"I don't want it."

"You're the only one here I trust, Jenny, so I'm proposing you whether you like it or not."

Brian and David were aghast at the announcement. Jennifer as chairman? The idea was ridiculous. Confronted by Carter, they refused to admit that their objection was based on the fact that she was neither a man nor a Hammond. Carter persisted in wanting to know the reason.

"The chairman of the board is the managing director and I'm not even prepared to consider it," said David.

"Give me a reason," Carter insisted.

"Ted's not here, for one thing."

"Because I'm not your brother?"

"Brothers or not," Brian broke in, "I for one am quite happy with Ted as chairman, whether you like it or not."

"Are you happy to see this firm go under?" Carter laid it on the line. "Transport companies are going to the wall every week through extending too much credit. The Parker debt was allowed to build up because Ted didn't want to upset an old mate. That makes him directly responsible."

"And he's gone personally to sort it out."

"Have you heard from him?"

"There's hardly been time...."

"All right. I'll give him another twenty-four hours," Carter looked at his watch. "Then I want that board meeting."

Brian and David looked at each other. Without Edward, they were floundering. Jennifer for chairman? The idea was preposterous. But suppose Edward didn't get back in time, then what? They invited Jennifer to join them for a drink at Brian's house that evening. Carter was not invited.

So both sides were competing for her favours. It gave her a pleasant feeling of power. At the same time, Jennifer tried to look at the position objectively. Any sentimentality vis-a-vis Hammond Transport was no longer relevant. It had changed from what it had been. It was no longer a one-man business but a growing company. It could no longer command that same unswerving personal loyalty. Harry Carter was a parvenu, a wheeler-dealer. Robert Hammond would not have tolerated him. But he was in situ. He was smart and he had been proved right on a number of occasions when the Hammonds were wrong. She reserved judgment.

Brian kicked off by asking her whether she was going to stand for the chair. She said that she wasn't. David asked whether this meant she disapproved of the move. She answered that she did – in the absence of Ted.

"But not if he were present?"

"Harry has a reasonable grievance," she observed. "He was put in charge of the warehouse in his absence."

"But if you're not prepared to stand," said Brian, "that's the end of it."

"I doubt it," said David. "I think he's putting Jenny up as a front. If we reject that, he'll offer himself."

"God forbid!" That thought hadn't occurred to Brian.

Jennifer thought carefully. "There's nothing to say that Ted's in the chair for life."

David wheeled on her. "Does that mean you back Carter?"

"If I thought it was good for the firm, yes."

"Jenny, you can't be serious," Brian said.

"Why not? It might make a change to have a chairman who isn't part of the family."

This was serious. David and Brian exchanged glances. A raised eyebrow from Brian gave David the go-ahead.

"You do realise he's been jockeying for this ever since he came here?"

"If you mean he's ambitious, I know," Jennifer answered. "But perhaps we could do with a little more ambition in this firm and a little less nepotism."

The blow went home. David was very cool. "Well you'd better know, Jenny, that neither of us is going to support."

"That's what I mean by nepotism."

"So you've both got a fight on your hands," David continued.

"That's all right," Jennifer got up. There was nothing more to say.

Harry Carter guessed that Tom Parker would be in one of three places: Albania, Tangiers or Monaco. Brian wondered how he knew. It was, in fact, Monaco. Edward was on his way there now.

"You know what's common to those three places?" Harry was rubbing salt in the wounds now. "They have no extradition treaties with Britain. And Parker's money will all be in Switzerland. I said I'd give Ted twenty-four hours. Now, when do I get that meeting?"

Brian delayed. "You don't."

"Brian," Carter said patiently. "Do you have another job lined up, or private means? Because I'm interested to know what you plan to do when Hammonds collapses."

"It's not going to collapse," Brian said stoutly.

Carter spoke slowly as though hoping to drive the significance of his words one by one into his listeners' heads. "It is going into bankruptcy unless someone takes a firm hand right now. For God's sake stop burying your head in the sand."

Carter got his board meeting.

He liked the feel of the chair. Until he had joined Hammonds, he had always run his own show. He listened to the minutes of the last meeting with pleasure. They were accepted and signed. Now he could get on to the real business of the day.

"You can get out of my chair," Edward walked in to the room. He had come straight from the airport.

"Just keeping it warm for you, Ted." Carter smiled at him sincerely.

Brian and David felt embarrassed. Edward looked furious.

"On whose authority do you call a board meeting in my absence?"

"Democratic decision." Carter was the only one capable of speech.

"I see. Right, Brian, I want you in my office immediately."

Without waiting for an answer, Edward turned and left. Brian got up to follow him. The board meeting was over.

Brian stammered out his apologies to Edward. Edward was

unpleasant. He accused them of scheming behind his back. He told Brian Carter was not running the company and never would. Brian agreed. To change the subject, he asked whether Edward had tracked down Parker.

Finding him had been the only successful part of the operation. The news was bad. Parker was going bankrupt. He couldn't settle his debt. Edward was stopping deliveries straight away and filing suit in the bankruptcy court. He wanted a meeting with Brian and David privately. He was leaving out Jennifer. She was all too kindly disposed towards Carter. Edward wanted to get rid of him.

The Hammond brothers met at Brian's house which was becoming an extension of the board room these days, Brian thought, as he poured drinks. He could set it against tax if things went on like this.

In principle, the brothers were all for getting rid of Carter. In practice, it was not so simple. They agreed he was trying to take over. They knew he was smart enough to out-manoeuvre them. But what action could they take?

Edward had three propositions to put to Carter. He could take the job of warehouse manager and start working for his living. He could take his vans and clear off. Or Hammonds could buy him out.

"We don't have the money to buy him out, Ted," Brian said.

"Then we'll have to find it."

Edward's memorandum explaining these alternatives was no surprise to Carter. They met the following afternoon.

"Well, what's it to be?" Edward asked.

"I don't like threats, Ted."

"They're proposals."

"When someone threatens me, my first reaction is to smack him in the teeth. But that wouldn't be fitting behaviour for a director of Hammond Transport, would it? So, I suppose we'll have to pretend we're gentlemen and bargain."

"I gave you three alternatives."

Carter corrected him. "One proposition, two alternatives. Let's take the first one. You know just what you can do with your warehouse job, don't you? Right up your exhaust pipe, mate. Second. Take my vans out of it. Now, that's one of your bright ideas, isn't it. But you'll get no support for it. Not even from your brothers. Those vans will be showing a profit over the next twelve months. Pull them out now and you've got a substantial loss. So we'll forget that one, too, shall we? So that leaves the golden handshake."

It was the proposal Edward hoped he would accept. "If you want out," he said, trying to be clever.

"I don't want out, mate. I'm happy here. But if you want *me* out, it's going to cost you."

"How much?"

"Ten years' salary in a lump sum, taking into account annual increments and an agreed figure to compensate for depreciation of the pound."

Edward laughed out loud. "Now what about a serious proposition?"

"Oh, I'm serious, mate. If you want to get rid of me then you'll just have to raise the money, won't you?"

The directors had to meet again to discuss Carter's compensation payment. After much haggling, they arrived at a sum equal to five years' salary. Carter wanted it in cash. It was a lot of money to find.

CHAPTER TWENTY-FOUR

A strange period now followed. When things are at their lowest ebb and there is nothing to lose, one can crystallise what one really wants. Life becomes like a fallow field and you decide what you want to put into it.

Once Edward had decided he wanted to get rid of Carter, his life became simpler because there was only one course of action open to him: to raise the money. At the moment it seemed an impossible task but at least it was a definite goal.

Nancy Lincoln had made up her mind, too. She had faced up to the problem of Edward and decided that he was not the man for her. Her husband was not the man for her, either, but he was her husband. She was responsible for him. She wasn't responsible for Edward yet. She explained this to Edward. Their parting was not acrimonious. They respected each other. Edward knew she was right. They did not have the relationship he and Jennifer had had. It was second-best. And second-best was no longer good enough.

Ann Hammond had decided what she wanted. Life in the country bored her. There was no other man on the scene. She had met more people when she was living the life of a married woman. She had had a bad shock when Brian started going out with Pamela Graham. She felt she had prepared the ground there carefully. Pamela Graham should by now have broken off the relationship. Ann telephoned Brian.

Brian was feeling lonely again. He felt now that he had a double failure on his hands. Ann's suggestion that they have a day out together without the children was just what he needed.

It was a magnificent day. The sun shone, Ann looked lovely and they walked and talked as they never had before. Ann was worried about the children. She told him how upset they were after his visits. He felt a little guilty. Somehow it was implied that it was his fault.

And Ann was applying for a job. She was to be interviewed the following week. Brian suggested they have dinner afterwards and she could tell him all about it. She radiated pleasure at the invitation.

There wasn't actually an interview. But Ann had been thinking about a job. Anything to get out and meet people. She shopped, bought a new dress which she kept on and drove over to meet Brian at the house. They had a drink and chatted. Slightly ill at ease with each other, it was as though it were their first date. Brian admired her dress. Ann asked where they were going to dinner.

They were booked at The Trellis. Ann acted slightly alarmed. She wondered whether Brian had ever taken Miss Graham there. It had been *their* place and she would be so embarrassed if he had. Brian reassured her. He would never take another woman to The Trellis. He didn't notice Ann's smile.

Dinner was a success. Ann didn't cross-examine him about his thoughts, didn't argue with him about points of principle. She was so restful. She just sat, looked beautiful and flattered him outrageously. He invited her to have a liqueur at home before she left.

"Darling," she reached up and put her arms around him. "I want to thank you for the best dinner I've ever had."

She was soft and pliant in his arms. He remembered every curve, every bone of her body. It had been a long time. He wanted her. But first he had to find out . . .

"Ann, are you lonely?"

"Yes," she whispered, nuzzling his ear. "Are you?"

"Yes."

"Then what do we do about it?" Ann wanted him to make the first move.

"We could see each other more often."

That wasn't quite good enough. "How much more often?"

"Does one make the same mistake twice?" Brian wanted reassurance.

"We could pretend we've just met."

Brian laughed. It was another of Ann's delicious games. She was a child really. A lovable, spoiled child. "And Nigel and Carol, where did they come from?"

"Oh, they were just around."

"We'd have to be very careful this time."

"Walk on tiptoes for a while." Her hand had snuggled up under his shirt and she was stroking his back. He loved it.

"I feel like getting in the car right now and driving down through the night to collect your things."

"My things are already upstairs, darling."

Brian was taken aback. For a moment he was annoyed. But then her hands moved round, stroking him, exciting him. She was murmuring endearments. She loved him. She wanted him. Ann had come back.

David had proposed to Jill in a weak moment. He recognised that. But having taken the step, he was reasonably contented. He shrugged off the uneasy feeling that he had been manoeuvred into it. It was just Julie's jealousy which had made her say that. But he knew now that he couldn't marry her.

Jill had had a letter from her late father's solicitor. The will had been declared. She was an heiress.

"How much, darling?" he asked casually.

"About a quarter of a million."

David couldn't believe it. She was terribly rich. If he married her now, everything he did would be totally unnecessary. His earnings, by comparison, would be pocket money. But what he was really afraid of was that the money would give Jill power over him. He would be well and truly trapped.

Jill had been afraid of this but she had worked out her strategy.

"Oh well," she sighed. "It looks as though I'll have to find myself another husband."

"That shouldn't pose a problem," David said sourly. "They'll be lining up at your door."

"Oh but it does pose a problem. You see I have to choose someone who doesn't just want me for my money. And how will I know?"

"Poor little rich girl," David mocked.

"On the other hand, of course, I could hang on to you and give all my money to charity. Would that make you feel better?"

"Which charity?"

"Does it matter? Pick one out of the book."

"No need to give it all," David backed down slightly. After

all, he couldn't be responsible for Jill's giving away all her money and it would be nice to afford a decent flat.

"No? Then how much do you think?"

"It's not for me to say."

"But it is, darling. I have to fix a figure at which I'm acceptable to you."

David couldn't discuss it in these terms. Jill was being altogether too flippant. He suggested she kept the money and went round the world. She didn't want to go round the world. He suggested they break off the engagement for six months and think things over.

"Have you got a pen?" Jill asked. Mystified, he handed his over. She made some rapid calculations. "Two hundred and fifty thousand pounds invested at, say, nine per cent over six months . . . I shall then be worth ten thousand more. Won't that make it even harder?"

"Jill, please try to see it my way . . ."

Jill squeezed a tear. "You're not in love with me."

"I *am* in love with you."

"In sickness and in health?"

"Yes."

She pounced. "For richer for poorer?"

"Yes."

"Problem solved." She kissed him. "Darling, you've passed all the tests. I accept you."

The trap closed.

Jill no longer had a fiance; she had a future husband. She went to see her future mother-in-law. They had a long talk together. Mary, of course, had been delighted with the news of the engagement. Jill was all she had dreamed of. They lunched together, shopped together. They got on very well indeed. They both loved David. This time Mary knew she wasn't losing a son, she was gaining a daughter.

After their chat, Mary suggested that Jill wait for Edward. They would be able to have a quiet discussion with nobody to disturb them.

Edward was surprised that Jill wanted to speak to him. When she told him why, he was stunned. She was offering him the money to buy out Carter.

"What on earth would you want to do that for?"

"I don't. But if it would help things at all, I thought I could put money in the firm."

"How much?"

"However much you need. Then there's this Parker debt as well, I believe. How much would it take to put the firm on its feet again?"

Edward was reeling under the impact of what she was saying. He had been sweating blood. His talk of buying out Carter was threatening to become empty, embarrassing. And here was Jill, looking as though butter wouldn't melt in her mouth, offering him salvation in hard cash.

Mary came in with coffee. She looked at Edward. Knew what he was thinking.

"I had nothing to do with this, Edward. It's entirely Jill's idea. She is now a wealthy young woman."

"Are you talking about a loan, Jill?"

"No. I'd just like to help out. But you can use it as collateral for a loan if you like. I don't fully understand these things."

Edward had a sudden thought. "And does David go along with this?"

"It had nothing to do with David," his mother said. "It's Jill's money."

"I don't understand, Jill. I really don't. Why should you do this?"

"I'd like to make sure my future husband has a job to go to. Otherwise he'll be getting under my feet all day and feeling terribly guilty. And that would never work out."

It had all been cooked up by his mother, of course. She had approved of the idea for two reasons. The money would save Hammonds by getting rid of Carter. And once the money was ploughed into the firm, there would be no getting out of the marriage for David. He would be totally committed.

Edward lingered only on the first reason. Hammonds would be saved. Forget David and his pride. It didn't matter where the money came from. He'd said that from the beginning. He'd talk David into it if Jill couldn't. Anyway, she was practically a Hammond now. There was no reason not to take the money.

CHAPTER TWENTY-FIVE

If Edward was prepared to save Hammonds and get rid of Carter at any price, his fellow-directors weren't. With the exception of Carter, of course, who had already planned how to spend the money. Always provided that Edward had managed to raise it.

They were together at yet another board meeting. Edward outlined the situation for them once more. He did not feel that Carter's continued presence on the board was desirable and, of the three proposals put to him, Carter had chosen the golden handshake.

Brian felt weary. Edward was living in cloud-cuckoo land if he really thought he could raise the money to buy out Carter. He said so. Edward asked David to explain.

David was not happy. He did not like the idea of Jill's being a rich woman, even worse was the thought of her ploughing the money into Hammonds. He delivered his account in a flat, miserable voice.

"Jill's father died a while ago. He was a fairly wealthy man. Jill is a major beneficiary under his will. She is prepared to back us."

It was like sighting land after drifting for days upon the sea. And equally unlikely. Brian interrupted.

"Back us to what extent?"

"All we need to see us through and to buy Carter out. There's enough."

Jennifer saw problems. "If she injects money into the company, won't she want a shareholding in return? That would virtually give you control, David."

"No," David reassured her. "She wouldn't be buying in. She would guarantee our present and future necessary loans and overdrafts, that's all."

"It would have to be a binding arrangement," Brian was back in his accountant's hat. "There'd be an element of risk. She could lose her money."

"She's prepared for that. She has faith in us all." David's voice was tinged with irony.

Only Carter looked pleased. He was staring at David in open admiration. What a coup to bring off! The guy must be great in bed!

"Boy, that's a convenient marriage you're making, Dave. Congratulations."

Brian was working out calculations in his head. It would work, all right, no question of that. With such a guarantee, they could continue normal operations, get themselves back on an even keel, buy out Carter. But he didn't like it. He said so.

"I don't like it either," said Jennifer. "I'm sorry, David."

"Don't worry. I expect I like it even less than you do."

"It's too personal," said Jennifer.

"Exactly," said Brian. "It's not a business proposition. It's a private favour for no other reason than . . ." He broke off, unwilling to insult David.

"No other reason than a convenient marriage," David quoted Carter's words. That's what they were all saying to themselves. He might as well say it out loud.

"Who cares?" said Carter. "If it gets you out of a hole?"

"I do," said David.

Edward looked round. They weren't buying it. Jennifer and Brian wouldn't offer up David as a sacrifice. Well, he would. It was time they had some straight talking. Funny, really, this meeting was to get rid of Carter and he and Carter were the only people here who spoke the same language. Who knew that the business always comes first.

"Right," he said. "I agree with everything you say. Have you got an alternative?"

They hadn't. Brian had exhausted every possible lead and source. There was no other money forthcoming.

"We'd be under an obligation to Jill," said Jennifer.

"She'll be a Hammond soon," Edward retorted. It was a barbed statement.

"Oh, that, of course, makes it different." Jennifer was stung.

"Yes, it does," said Edward. "This way we can keep the company afloat."

"There must be something else we can do," Jennifer insisted.

"There is," Edward paused. "We can go into liquidation. Let's vote. All those in favour of accepting the offer."

Carter was the only one to raise his hand.

"I think I should abstain," said David.

"My vote goes in favour," said Edward. "That makes two. Those against."

Edward looked at Brian.

"I'm abstaining," Brian muttered.

"Me, too," said Jennifer.

"Right. Carried." Carter grinned happily.

"Not yet it isn't." Edward said. "I'm disregarding that vote."

"You can't do that!" Carter could see his money vanishing.

"I've done it," Edward announced calmly. He was superbly in control now. Tough. Determined. He looked round the table. "Now then. This is probably the most important decision we've ever taken. Whether Hammond Transport lives or dies. If you three feel strongly about it, vote against. You can defeat this proposal, if you want to, by three to two. But I want to see your hands up this time, one way or the other. Right. Again. All those in favour."

Carter's hand shot up. He stared at them as though willing them to follow his lead. Very reluctantly, Brian raised his hand. Then Jennifer raised hers. Finally David raised his. It was carried unanimously.

Edward looked round at them all. He had had to do it. They had to put up a united front on an issue as big as this. He wondered fleetingly what he would have done if they had voted against. "Well," he said unsmiling. "We're still in business."

"Yes," Jennifer blurted out. "By courtesy of the new recruit to the Hammond family."

The day Harry Carter collected his money, he went shopping. He bought presents for his ex-fellow directors of Hammonds.

He called to Brian's office first. He felt grateful to Brian. He had got the wheels turning fast. The documents had been drawn up and payment made in record time. Carter did not put this down to vulgar haste to get rid of him but to Brian's efficiency.

"I'm glad we got it well sorted out with no ill feelings, Brian. Here, I've got a farewell gift for you." He handed the amazed Brian a small package. "It's a pen. Supposed to have five miles of ink in it so that should see you through some figuring. It's solid silver so if you don't want it, you can always hock it." Carter paused. "Talking about that, you fellows are in hock to your young brother now, you know that, don't you? And he's in hock to his little bride. I hope they're happy, that's all, because he can't very well walk out on her now, can he?" He grinned again and left.

David got two presents. A travelling alarm clock for himself. "For when you're going round the country digging up all that new business," Carter explained. And a wedding present. This was a pair of egg coddlers in genuine porcelain. If he couldn't use them, it was unlikely they were worth hocking but on the other hand, they would make nice ornaments.

Edward was presented with a large box of decent cigars. Carter accepted one for himself. He also gave Edward some good advice.

"I made a mistake, Ted. I picked out Hammond Transport as the right firm for me, not too big yet but ready to boom, go public in a year or two maybe and then there'd be real money around. But I was wrong. It's just a family business and I haven't got the time to sort you lot out. So I'd rather make what I can on the deal and move on. But I'll tell you this, Ted. You could be a big man except you've got one handicap. You're too honest. Shake that off and you'll be a millionaire yet."

Edward thanked him for the cigars.

Jennifer received an enormous bouquet of the most beautiful flowers. There was a card attached. "With respect and affection. Always yours. Harry."

She smiled at him. "Harry's the one who gives flowers. Carter's the one who sets people up and takes what he wants."

Carter was unrepentant. "The odds were even, Jenny. Four of you and one of me."

"I told you before. I prefer a few rules."

"That's your weakness. There's only one thing I regret about it. You."

"Harry," said Jennifer. "You used me."

"Only to the extent that you wanted to be used."

Jennifer was silent for a moment, thinking. Harry was right. And he had the guts to admit it. To speak out.

"There could have been something between you and me, Jenny. You know it and I know it. If a few things had been different, well – who knows? But I'll tell you this. I'll remember you long after I've forgotten all about Hammond Transport."

"I suppose that's the ultimate compliment," she said lightly.

Harry came up to her and took her in his arms. He kissed her full on the lips, hungrily. For a moment, she responded then pulled away. Maybe if things had been different. But they weren't. She loved Edward.

Carter had bought flowers for Mary Hammond. They were the same as he had bought for Jennifer. The card was the same, too. His reception was not, however, the same.

Harry Carter had caused her family trouble. Anyone who caused her family the slightest discomfort was Mary Hammond's implacable enemy. She read Carter's card in silence. Then she turned and gave him her opinion.

"It seems to me, Mr. Carter, that you measure everything in terms of money. You are motivated entirely by self-interest, you have no consideration for other people whatever. In all your dealings with my family, you have been concerned with your own advantage from beginning to end. You appear to have made money out of it but you will find there are certain things money cannot buy." She thrust the flowers back at him.

Carter was upset. He had a great esteem for Mary Hammond. He regarded her as an example of what he privately termed "real English lady". To discover that someone he respected had no respect for him was a considerable blow. He even tried to explain himself.

"You've got it wrong, Mrs. Hammond. You don't understand business, that's what it is," he stammered.

"If business means lying and cheating and grabbing, I don't wish to understand it, Mr. Carter. I have no respect for you nor do I want you in my house."

He left in a hurry.

Mary was delighted he had gone from Hammonds. Now it was just the family again. Or almost. If only he had taken that odious Kingsley woman with him.

CHAPTER TWENTY-SIX

The wedding service went off without a hitch. Jill looked radiant. Edward remembered the ring. And the two child attendants managed not to tread on the bride's train. Mary Hammond shed a few tears. She was happy.

It was done. David smiled at Jill as they walked back down the aisle together. Man and wife. Mr. and Mrs. David Hammond. It had a good ring.

The first person he saw as they came out of the church door was Julie. She was taking photographs. She instructed them to smile at her. Jill, the professional model, took up the model bride pose. David's face froze.

Julie came up to them. She kissed David.

"Congratulations." She didn't look as though she meant it.

Jill moved away to pose for the photographer David had employed.

David felt sick. What mischief was Julie cooking up? She handed him a silk scarf.

"This is Jill's. She left it in your flat. I took it by mistake last night."

Last night. He had let it happen again. Julie had deliberately found out where he was holding his stag party. She had turned up. He had invited her for a drink. She hadn't joined them. Not then. She had arrived later at his flat. He had given her a drink but hadn't joined her. He had told her to get out of his flat, to get out of his life. He had meant it. But he couldn't resist her. She had told him he never would be able to. But it wasn't true. He was married now. The Julies of the world were finished as far as he was concerned. He moved towards Jill and took her arm possessively.

Bill Riley was wearing his best suit and a new silk tie. He looked around the guests with approval. A fair old sprinkling of top hats and tails. There was still a good bit of money around. Hammonds seemed to have pulled through despite the rumours that had been flying around for the last few weeks. He was glad Carter had gone. He'd caused nothing but trouble. David had done well for himself. She was a pretty lass and no mistake. Rich, too. From what they said, she'd had a bit to do with the sudden change in fortunes. Mary Hammond must be pleased. She hadn't stopped smiling except to cry a bit. Still, women did that at weddings. She'd be looking forward to grandchildren, no doubt. They'd help to make her life less lonely in that big house of hers. Certainly his own missus set store by their grandchildren. She enjoyed them more than she'd enjoyed her own, he reckoned.

Mary Hammond was pleased. It was her day almost as much as Jill's. The only small cloud on the horizon was the presence of Miss Kingsley. Mary smiled and waved at Barbara. She didn't know how that woman had had the nerve to show her face here.

Jennifer had not wanted to come but David had insisted. He had pointed out that Barbara was his half-sister but it wasn't just a case of duty. He wanted them both there. Jennifer had agreed to come to the ceremony but refused the invitation to the reception.

Jennifer was looking beautiful, Edward thought. If only it had been their wedding day. Not that he would succumb to this form of civilised torture; he felt an absolute fool in this rig-out. Top hats! Jennifer started to move away. He rushed up to her.

"Jenny, hang on, would you?"

"We're not going on," she explained.

"No, but wait." Edward was called to join in the group pictures.

The family stood and smiled. Smiled and stood. Ann was bored. She looked at them all. Not unlike the last occasion we were all together, she thought. Except that was a funeral, not a wedding. Not that there was much difference, really. She was already tiring of playing house again. Cosy domesticity washed down with medium sherry to a background of Mahler. There must be something else to life. Births, christenings, weddings, funerals. And, in between, long boring stretches to be filled. Brian, beside her, sensed her boredom. He smiled at her nervously. She smiled exquisitely for the photographer.

It was over. The pictures had all been taken. The bride and groom got into their car. The last handful of confetti was poured over David's head by Julie. The look in her eyes told him it might as well be coals of fire.

Edward ushered his mother into her car. He didn't join her. He told her that he would catch up with her later at the reception. Mary leaned forward to remonstrate with him but he closed the door firmly against her protests.

As her car moved away, she watched him walk over to join Jennifer Kingsley and Barbara. He had an arm round each of them. Mary leaned back. Her day had been spoiled.

Edward smiled at Barbara. She grinned back. Thank heavens they'd seen sense at last. For a terrible time, she had thought Jennifer was considering Harry Carter. If Edward was around again, she could think of what she was going to do next. Travel a bit maybe. She wasn't sure about art school any more. Nicholas had kind of spoiled things there. That hurt had lessened, too. She'd get over him.

Jennifer was happy. Edward's arm round her felt good. Right. They had made silly mistakes. There was the odd crack in their relationship now but it would mend given time. And they had time. All the time in the world together.

"Come on," Edward said. "I'll take you home."